The New Agent

by

Albert Ryedale

This is a work of fiction. Names and characters are the product of the author's imagination and any resemblance to actual persons, living or dead, is entirely coincidental.

ISBN: 978-1-326-81735-0

PublishNation
www.publishnation.co.uk

To Dishy

Chapter 1

The bell of the village church lazily begins to ring out eleven chimes on this peaceful Sunday morning in Little Foxwood. Somewhere in the distance there is the faint knock of leather on willow followed by polite applause, but not much else disturbs the tranquillity of this charming village in the heart of the Cotswolds. June has arrived in a blaze of colour and splendour, and swallows and dragonflies add their own grace and beauty to this delightful pastoral scene that could rival the finest Constable masterpiece.

This however is no ordinary Sunday. The village green has become the venue for the Festival of Transport, and people from miles around and from all walks of life have congregated here for this very special occasion. All year the enthusiastic entrants have been preparing for this annual event, having spent many hours locked inside a shed or garage when snow was falling outside, fervently repairing, restoring and rebuilding their own personal labour of love. Considerable anxiety has been experienced by classic vehicle owners up and down the country, as they struggled to get their pride and joy to the show on time. And now the big day has arrived.

All morning strange vehicles of every shape and size have been arriving, and some owners have already taken out the folding chairs from the boot and have settled behind their car, tractor or steam engine with a flask of tea. Among the exhibits a 1913 Rolls Royce Silver Ghost sits majestically between a 1949 Triumph Roadster with a dickey seat at the rear, and a spectacular American 1958 Buick Roadmaster, resplendent in two tone sky blue and white, with flamboyant curves and fins, and a dazzling display of sparkling chrome.

To the right there is a fine collection of motorbikes, with some well-restored examples of BSA, Norton, AJS, and even a 1925 Brough Superior. Maybe Lawrence of Arabia once owned this bike. Farther along there is a line of curious machines which weren't meant to travel. These are stationary engines, built for farm work; threshing corn or producing electric light. Next to a wheezing and spluttering static engine an owner sits with as much pride as if he had brought along a Bugatti Royale. The Banbury Brass Band, invited to play for the occasion, starts its repertoire with a selection of popular songs.

Classic tractors are on display, as are military vehicles; jeeps, scout cars and a half-track in desert camouflage that might have seen active service in Tobruk. A nineteenth century steam-driven traction engine, gloriously restored with gleaming brass, is receiving much admiration from the public who are happily wandering around the village green with their children on this special Sunday.

Some stalls are selling confectionary, old magazines, craftwork, tools and polish, and some vendors have laid out all sorts of rusty parts of cars; axles, gear boxes, crankshafts, and one enthusiast who had been searching for a trunnion for his Frogeye Sprite considers himself a very lucky man.

The light chatter and laughter of children becomes increasingly drowned out by a very loud roar overhead. Everyone looks up in wonder to see what is causing this deafening noise. There, above and just away from the event below, the large, dark shape of a jet comes into view. Surely this can't be here for the show, people start saying to their wives and friends. Its undercarriage is already lowered, as if about to land. Now it is possible to identify the warplane by the half-moon air intakes. It's a Hawker Harrier Jump Jet. People stand in awe as the unbelievable sight of this iconic British fighter seems to sail in slow motion above them. It passes overhead and goes on to land in a quiet corner of the green, next to the village.

In the centre of the show two men are looking under the bonnet of a navy blue and cream 1929 Cadillac with wide running boards and large staring headlights mounted on a bar across the radiator. It boasts wire wheels with white wall tyres and wing-mounted spare wheel. The bonnet opens from one side and the owner has started up the engine for the fellow enthusiast. At a glance it's easy to tell the owner as he has dressed up for the occasion in a dark, double-breasted chalk-stripe suit, white spats, and a light grey fedora with a black band. The outfit is complete with black shirt and white tie.

A row of vintage lorries, with immaculate sign-writing on their doors stand proudly alongside fire engines, and firemen are only too willing to help children into the cab to ring the fire bell. People stroll around casually, with some stopping for an ice cream or a hotdog, or better still a visit to the beer tent.

Suddenly the back door of an old cream Daimler ambulance, in a line with police cars from a bygone age bursts open and six men pour out, each dressed in black and carrying a machine gun. They walk hurriedly through the show towards the section for steam engines. As they approach, the middle-aged man in checked shirt and cord trousers, sitting aloft the traction engine with a small boy invites the child to blow the whistle of the historic vehicle.

As the terrorists draw nearer they begin shouting in some unknown language. A young woman who has been serving at the fudge stall, hands the bag of rum and raisin to a lady and reaches down under the counter. A man in kaftan, tie-dye tee shirt and Jesus sandals who is sitting in his folding chair behind a psychedelic VW Campervan quickly gets to his feet and opens the back door. The older man on the traction engine lowers the boy into the arms of his mother, as the men run up to him, shouting aggressively. People stand staring at this unfolding situation, not quite sure if it is part of the show. A second man, dressed in a lime green drape coat with black velvet collar, drainpipe trousers and hair slicked back, reaches for a parcel on the back seat of his Model A Ford hot rod, its supercharged V8 Chevy engine brazenly exposed. The six terrorists now surround the man on the traction engine shouting fanatically and pointing their machine guns at him. Another woman dressed as a clippie on a London Route Master bus opens a package from the luggage area at the back of the bus and hurries over to the scene.

The gang start firing machine guns into the air. People start screaming; mothers grab their children and run for cover, behind cars, trucks, tractors. One of the terrorists gets onto the traction engine and tries to pull the man down. A volley of shots rings out. The girl from the sweet counter shoots the man dead with an assault rifle. The others spin round towards the special officer, but the Teddy boy officer manages to pick off another terrorist with an M16 rifle.

The enthusiast at the Cadillac pulls out a pistol and tells the owner to shut the bonnet and get away from the car. Machine gun bullets pierce holes into the boiler of the traction engine and jets of steam hiss from the holes. The man gets off the saddle and hides beneath the Victorian machine. A fire fight has erupted between the terrorists and the undercover officers, as the gang continue to fire indiscriminately. The hippy officer steps out from behind the Campervan to deliver a volley of machine gun fire but he is gunned down by the terrorists as bullets smash through the windows of the dormobile and puncture holes in the bodywork. The Teddy boy in rock and roll attire suffers a similar fate in a hail of bullets when trying to reach the man under the traction engine. The terrorists manage to drag the man from under the steam engine with a machine gun held to his head. The Cadillac now races up to the four terrorists and while they spray bullets at the officers who have taken up positions behind vintage vehicles, the middle-aged man is forced into the back of the car. With two terrorists inside and the other two on the running boards clinging to the window frame as they fire, the Cadillac speeds over the grass and away from the show. The officer who is dressed as a bus conductress runs over to a man at the wheel of a spectacular Mack truck which is adorned with chrome and overhead spotlights.

"Follow the car!" she shouts up to him, and climbs up into the cab. Without a second's delay he starts the engine and the vertical twin exhausts of the truck start roaring and he reaches up to blast the horn. The truck speeds away to catch up with the Cadillac. The two vehicles race along the village green with people diving for cover as they pass. Now the officer can see where the car is heading. The Harrier is waiting at the edge of the green with its jet engine still running. Behind the fighter, some men who had been enjoying a quiet lunchtime pint at the Dog and Parrot are now standing motionless across the road with their glasses in their hands as the twenties Cadillac and Mack truck head at speed towards the Jump Jet. The terrorists continue to fire up at the right side of the truck as the woman officer fires back.

"Forget the car!" she shouts at the driver. "Ram the plane!"

The truck and car are neck and neck with machine guns blazing, as the truck driver heads for the front wheel of the plane. One smash would immobilise it. A ladder from the belly of the plane rests on the grass. The pilot has increased the engine speed ready for take-off. The men are across the street outside the pub. The truck is just about to ram the nose of the plane when two boys appear out of nowhere on bikes and pass right in front of the truck. The driver swerves to avoid them and misses the plane. He shoots off the green, across the road and smashes straight through the front of the pub, as the panic-stricken regulars flee for their lives. The truck crashes right through the windows and front wall of the pub and only the rear wheels can be seen through the cloud of dust, broken glass and rubble.

The terrorists have got into the fuselage with their captive, and the Harrier performs a perfect vertical take-off from the edge of the village green. The powerful downdraught of the engine propels the plane up above the rooftops and for a moment it hovers gracefully, and then with a deafening roar of thunder it shoots up into the sky and two seconds later it has gone.

Later that day Bentley arrives at MI6 headquarters, responding to an urgent request from his commanding officer, Hargreaves. When he reaches the office, the secretary tells him to go straight in.

"Ah, good afternoon Bentley", Hargreaves begins. "Good of you to get here so quickly".

"Afternoon sir", replies Bentley. "Something important?"

"We had an incident this morning at a classic car show in the Cotswolds", Hargreaves starts to explain.

"Oh no - don't tell me a bubble car's blown a gasket", Bentley jokes.

"I'm afraid it's more serious than that, Bentley", replies Hargreaves humourlessly.

"Sorry sir – do go on", Bentley says apologetically.

"A group of terrorists managed to stage an audacious coup to kidnap one of our scientists. They escaped with him in a Harrier that had been captured in the Middle East some time ago."

"What was he doing at a car show in the Cotswolds?" Bentley asks.

"One of his great passions was his beloved traction engine. He'd been restoring it for years and we never thought he was in any danger so I authorised that he could go. We had four undercover officers there, but they failed to prevent his capture", Hargreaves explains.

"What do they want with him?" Bentley asks.

"Honeyman had been working on a new style of nuclear bomb for quite a while and it was near completion. Somehow the terrorists found out about it and kidnapped him so he'd be forced to build it for them. If they get their hands on it, half of the Western world will be destroyed”.

“What’s different about this bomb?” Bentley questions.

“This bomb has no fall-out. Up until now fall-out has protected a nation against its enemy. If Pakistan dropped a bomb on India they would suffer from the fall-out too. After the explosion at the power station in Chernobyl in ’86 we had to slaughter sheep in this country. But without fall-out a country could reduce its neighbour to ruins with no cost to itself. North Korea could flatten Seoul and not affect any other country nearby. That is why it’s utterly imperative that we get Honeyman back before it’s too late. You’re booked on a flight to Baghdad tonight, and Bentley – you mustn’t fail”.

“Back or streaky?”

“I beg your pardon?”

“Bacon - are you listening? What kind of bacon do you want – we’ll be here all day at this rate. Back or streaky?”

“Back”, replies Gordon. “Or streaky”.

“For crying out loud!” his wife answers impatiently.

“Oh sorry dear”, Gordon says sheepishly. “I was deep in thought. What were you saying?”

“Oh, for Christ’s Sake! Shopping with you is a nightmare. If it was left to you there wouldn’t be a thing to eat in the house”.

Gordon wanders along the aisles of the supermarket behind his wife, Mabel as she throws things into the trolley.

“Come on, come on! Let’s get this done and get out of here”, she barks at him.

“Yes of course dear. Sorry – I was miles away”, Gordon replies meekly.

“If only that were true!” she replies bitterly.

Chapter 2

It's a stormy, late autumn day in Glasgow. People hurry along pavements, dodging traffic, rushing to their respective places of work. Flimsy umbrellas blow inside out as commuters step off buses and emerge from underground exits. On a day like this all that matters to the hapless employee is to get out of the tempest and into the shelter of a twenty storey office block. Then for the unpleasant sensation of drenched trousers clinging to legs under desks, and cold, wet feet because of those unsuitable summer shoes you chose to wear. From the seventeenth floor faint car horns can be heard somewhere in the howling wind, and car headlights are inconsequential white dots in the distance.

And so another day for Gordon, who stands in a grey suit looking down at the business world just coming to life. Shipping never was his idea of an interesting job, but for twenty years he has sat here in this same office without ever having been to sea. The only thing that happened was that ten years ago he had to give up the luxury of his own office and sit at his desk in an open-plan room with a hundred people. Phones ring, people shout, keyboards clatter and kettles boil. Nine o'clock on a Monday morning in October in Glasgow.

Gordon eventually turns his attention to late container deliveries on his computer and with a sigh of acceptance, opens the folder. Some delay leaving Southampton. Industrial dispute at Zeebrugge. No work permits for Filipino crew at Stavanger. More headaches to worry about. After a few minutes his phone rings. It's Edna, the manager's secretary.

"Oh good morning Gordon," she begins. "I wonder if you wouldn't mind popping along to see Mr Grainger. It won't take long."

"Yes of course Edna. I'll come right now," Gordon replies.

When he arrives at her desk she tells him to go straight into the boss's office. Gordon opens the door and inside Grainger is at his desk sifting through various documents.

"Gordon, good to see you – please take a seat", Grainger says as Gordon enters.

"Hello Walter – how are you?" asks Gordon.

"Oh just struggling along as usual. How's your mother? I heard she's had some rather ill health recently."

"Yes I'm afraid so. She had another stroke last night. It's pretty serious this time. I can't see her surviving this one."

"Oh dear", replies Walter. "I am really sorry to hear such bad news."

"Thanks –it's been a bit of a difficult time really. When you get to a certain age in life I suppose you can expect these things to happen"

"Which is why I asked you to pop in for a little chat this morning", Walter says in a more business-like manner. "You've probably heard about the woeful position the company's in".

"Well I've read in the paper that we have some financial difficulties at the moment. How serious is it?"

The mood becomes more sombre as Walter explains the situation. "You may have also heard that the company is having to lay off staff to try and keep costs down."

"What an awful state of affairs Walter. I would never have believed that a company that was once so prosperous is now making its employees redundant."

"And no one laments the situation more than I do Gordon. This company has been my life and the way things are going we'll be heading for administration in under a year."

Gordon steels himself and asks Walter, "Am I going to lose my job?"

"I can't lie to you Gordon," replies Walter. "You better prepare yourself if the axe is to fall."

Gordon takes a deep breath. "That would be a disaster. I've just taken on a huge mortgage. My wife insisted on a bigger house. I knew it was a mistake. If I lose my job I could be declared bankrupt. I wouldn't be able to get a job so easily at my age. I don't know what I'd do."

"Who knows Gordon – let's hope it doesn't come to that. These are challenging times to say the least. I thought it was right for me to warn you."

"Thanks for telling me Walter. I appreciate it.", replies Gordon.

Chapter 3

The flight to Manchester seems to take so long, and it's another dull an overcast day with drizzle in the air when Gordon finally arrives by taxi at the Western General Infirmary. The nurse on duty, who must still been in her teens is hanging patients' records at the end of the beds in Ward 9. He has come to visit his mother whom he believes would not recover from the stroke she had the day before. The nurse chats to the elderly ladies as she goes around the ward. She welcomes Gordon as he stands awkwardly at the door of the ward.

"Oh Gordon, how nice to see you. Your mother is next door. Please come with me and I'll take you to see her."

"Thank you. Is there any improvement?

"Maybe a slight improvement, but I must warn you she won't be able to respond or recognise you."

"Yes, okay."

The nurse takes Gordon along the corridor to a private ward where his mother is lying motionless. A sign which reads 'Nil by Mouth' hangs at the end of the bed. It is a pitiful sight to see his mother just staring vacantly and meaninglessly trying to move a hand in the air.

"Hello Kitty - here's your son – he's come to pay you a visit. Isn't that nice?" the nurse says cheerfully. "You can spend as long as you like with your mother," the nurse tells Gordon, trying to comfort him.

"Thank you – I don't suppose I'll have much to say."

"If you want anything, just let me know", the young nurse says and leaves them alone.

Gordon pulls up a chair by the bedside, and after a moment or two starts to speak.

"Hi Mum, how are you? Getting a bit chilly now we're into October. Heard you had a little stroke last night. Never mind though – can't be too serious. You'll be back on your feet in no time."

His mother shows no recognition. She just lies staring into space with her mouth gaping open. After a pause Gordon resumes his monologue.

"Things aren't going so well with me and Mabel these days. She's always irritable with me and criticises me every time she speaks to me. She never misses a chance to ridicule me. And then there's my job. That's a worry too, because they're going to be laying off staff soon and I might be one of them. My boss has already warned me."

Gordon realises he is beginning to give too much of his misfortunes away in front of his mother, and reins in his worries.

"Don't you worry about me though – I'll be fine. Everyone has trouble at work these days. We've just got to concentrate on you getting better as soon as possible. You'll be home again and pottering about the garden, and meeting the girls for coffee just like you used to. Everything'll be just fine, you wait and see. I'm going to look after you the way you looked after me. Remember when I was five or six you used to pick me up from school at lunchtime when the snow was falling and we'd go to that old café – what was it called - the Rendezvous, to keep warm and have some soup. Remember those days? Such a long time ago now…"

His mother tries to raise a hand, but continues to stare blankly. He wonders if she has heard any of what he said. Just then the nurse comes into the private ward.

"Well Kitty - wasn't that nice for Gordon to pop along to see you. He'll be back again tomorrow", the nurse says again to his mother in an upbeat manner.

"Okay – I better be going now. Maybe there'll be some improvement tomorrow."

"Well you just never know", the nurse says reassuringly.

"Bye Mum", he says to his mother who of course lies motionless. "You take care and I'll be back tomorrow." With a faint polite smile to the nurse, he leaves the private ward and makes his way along the corridor.

Chapter 4

At the front of the 737 the air hostess makes her way along the aisle carrying a tray supported by a strap around her neck, like an usherette selling ice cream in a cinema. She hands out free packets of confectionary to the passengers of the Lufthansa flight to Berlin with a smile and occasional few words. From his aisle seat Bentley observes her as she slowly approaches him. Of medium-to-tall stature at about five foot six with long blond hair, and wearing the company royal blue suit with the skirt a couple of inches above the knee, she slowly walks towards Bentley, who casually studies her shapely figure. Eventually she reaches his seat and asks him if he would like a small tube of the sweets which she is giving out. He looks up at her smiling blue eyes and accepts the packet.

"Love Hearts", he comments. "I haven't had these since I was a child. They used to have such innocent messages like 'Be Mine' and 'True Love'".

"Maybe you'll find a romantic message today", she replies with a smile. "Are you travelling to Berlin on business", she asks.

"Only for a few days and then I hope to do a bit of sight-seeing", he answers.

The plane is only half-full with no one sitting in the seats next to him. She turns to someone on the opposite side, and Bentley glances at her hourglass figure as she moves away.

He settles down again and has another sip of his gin and tonic. He looks down at the packet of Love Hearts on the table and decides to open it as he thinks about his assignment in Berlin. He tears away the wrapping from the small round paper tube which only contains about ten complimentary sweets. He exposes the first sweet and reads the simple message printed on it.

'THE MAN' is the strange message that he reads. How odd - must be some sort of misprint, he imagines as he pops the round, flat sweet into his mouth. It has a sweet, pleasant flavour which is confused by another sip of gin. Now he notices the next sweet in the packet. 'BEHIND YOU' is printed on the second sweet. His fingers tear away the paper wrapper and he pops the second one into his mouth. 'IS GOING' is the message on the third. He tears away the wrapper again and puts this one into his mouth. 'TO KILL YOU' is on the next sweet. His eyes move slowly upwards as he begins to comprehend the message.

He swallows the sweets, finishes his drink in one mouthful and puts up the table. He didn't notice who was sitting behind, but he can't look round now. All is quiet on the plane with just a few people reading books and magazines. He reaches under the seat. His fingers fumble for what is located there. He finds what he was looking for and quietly pulls out the inflatable life jacket. As if standing up to reach into the locker, he sees the man behind him. He is small, of middle-eastern appearance with a black beard, about thirty, and has his hands inside a small rucksack.

With a sudden lunge forward he forces the life jacket over the man's head and continues to manoeuvre it over his shoulders until it has been forced down to his elbows. The man struggles to free himself but in a second Bentley pulls the ripcord and the life jacket instantly blows up around the man's arms and waist. Bentley fastens the seat belt over the man's lap and he is immobilised. Some of the passengers gasp in surprise.

He reaches into the rucksack and pulls out a large ceremonial dagger with a curved blade and decorated hilt. The air hostess is already at the scene next to Bentley.

"He must have an over-inflated opinion of himself", he remarks to the girl.

"When you finish your business in Berlin, come and see me in Dusseldorf", she suggests as she hands a card with her number to Bentley.

"Thank you", Bentley replies. "I'd be delighted".

Chapter 5

Mabel has already had her breakfast when Gordon sits down at the table. The ads on the radio are too fast and too loud, but Mabel flips through a magazine while Gordon pours himself some cereal. Not a word passes between them while he eats his breakfast. He thinks about his mother, and wonders if it will be today when she passes away. Eventually, it is Mabel who makes the first comment.

"I'm going to a car showroom after I finish work. I can't bear to be seen in that old wreck any longer. It's just an embarrassment. It's high time we got a decent car, so I'm going to find out how much another car would cost."

"Well, it's not a good time right now to be buying a new car. I had to see Walter yesterday and he told me there was a real possibility of me being made redundant."

"Oh great – that's all we need. As if life wasn't bad enough, now you're going to lose your job. Well too bad, because we need a new car, and we'll just have to get a bank loan to pay for it. You'll just have to find another job that's all."

"I wish I could but it's not so easy these days, especially at my age," replies Gordon. "I was hoping by now I'd have got one of my novels published.

"Oh grow up for God's sake", snaps Mabel. "When are you going to give up this ridiculous fantasy that one day you'll be a famous writer? How many people are there out there who have some dream of being a writer? How many turn out to be JK Rowling? If you want to get on in this world you can forget those childish ideas and go out and get a proper job."

"It's always been an ambition of mine to be a writer instead of having to work in that boring shipping office."

"And then there's all those silly inventions. You spend hours in Maplin's looking for some electronic gadget to solder together. Gordon Scrimgeour – Glasgow's answer to Thomas Edison. The famous inventor of the cat flap that opens automatically when the cat miaows. The only trouble is, you forgot to tell the cat. It's not exactly the Dyson vacuum cleaner, is it? Look, I've got to go to work. Get your own dinner when you get in."

She gets up and starts running a plate under the tap.

"I saw mum yesterday. She had another stroke. I think she's only got days to go," Gordon tells Mabel as she puts a few things into her handbag.

"Has she made out a will?" Mabel asks.

"Yes – everything was taken care of before she had the strokes," Gordon tells her.

"Who are the beneficiaries?"

"Everything in her estate will go to me."

"Well, well – things aren't quite so bleak after all. We can get a brand new car once she kicks the bucket."

The front door slams as Gordon sits in the kitchen a little longer looking at the gathering clouds before he has to get ready to make his way to the station for another tedious day in shipping.

Chapter 6

It's busy and noisy as usual in the open plan shipping office in the Anderston area of Glasgow. Julie and Helga, two young women who work in the same department as Gordon are gossiping quietly after hearing some news of his situation.

"I hear his mother's only got a couple of days till she pops her clogs," Julie begins, filing a nail. "She had some stroke or something."

"Yeah I was hearing," Helga replies. "Well they've gotta go sooner or later. The older they get, the more of a nuisance they are."

"Have you heard about his wife though?" Julie asks. "They say she's screwing some other guy and everyone knows about it except Gordon – and his mother on her deathbed too. Wait until he finds out – he'll go mental."

"He fancies himself as a bit of a writer of spy novels, but his books must be pretty rubbish – every publisher in Britain's turned him down," Helga says to Julie.

"He's not bad looking though for a guy in his fifties, and still got a good head of hair," Julie remarks.

"Yeah, still got his dark hair, and he's tall and slim, so his old cow of a wife should consider herself lucky".

"Watch out – here he comes now."

"Morning Gordon," the secretaries say as he goes to his desk.

"Morning Julie, Helga – how are you this morning?"

"We're fine thanks. How's your mum - any change?" Helga enquires.

"Well, not so good to be honest," he replies. "It's not looking so good."

"That's a real shame," replies Julie, trying to appear sympathetic.

Gordon sits at his desk, and boots up his computer.

"And how's your wife – Mabel, isn't it?" asks Helga, trying to glean some more saucy bits of gossip.

"She's fine," he answers.

"Must be great to be happily married and be devoted to just the one person," Julie mocks without him knowing.

“Well it’s not all plain sailing you know Julie. There are ups and downs in a marriage.”

“Well it certainly looks like it,” observes Helga, and winks at Julie.

Gordon’s phone rings. It’s Edna. She asks Gordon if he could pop in to see Grainger. When he hangs up he wonders if this is the moment he’s been dreading. He stands slowly and takes a deep breath. He goes into Grainger’s office. There are no pleasantries this morning. The mood is gloomy.

“I’ve been given a list by Head Office of those who are being made redundant, and I regret to inform you that your name is on the list. I can only offer you my greatest sympathy that it has come to this, at a time when you mother is gravely ill,” Grainger reluctantly tells Gordon.

Gordon sighs and looks dejected as he gazes at the floor. “I see. So my time has come. Do I continue working till the end of the month?”

“Well Gordon, you know how Management handle redundancies,” Grainger explains. “They want you to clear your desk right away and leave as soon as possible. I can only offer you my sincere commiserations.”

Gordon is shocked by the news. The colour fades from his face as he makes his way back to his desk. A security man with a large cardboard box is waiting for him. The girls look over, slowly catching on to what is happening. It seems everyone in the room is staring at him as he fumbles with papers and documents, trying hard not to show any emotion. The office becomes silent, with no one typing or chatting. He tries to act in a methodical, dignified manner, but he wants to just throw everything he has into the box and run out of the office.

“Good luck Gordon,” the girls say. Gordon tries to force a smile, but the lump in his throat prevents him from replying verbally. He just lifts his raincoat from the coat stand, nods as he clutches his box, and walks to the lift with the security guard. He feels as if he is being marched to the door like a common criminal. The office is deathly quiet as he walks out of the office for the last time.

Chapter 7

'Mind the gap', a tannoyed voice warns passengers at Westerton station as the doors open and people alight. All the way home on the train Gordon was shocked at being made redundant. This happens to other people, never to you. It's always someone else's problem. Now it's Gordon's problem. The doors close and the train is on its way again. He thinks about how he can manage now – things were already difficult and now Mabel wants a new car. His mind races. His heart pounds as he walks out of Bearsden station and up the hill to his house. What'll he do now? He'll never get another job at his age.

It's only eleven o'clock, but he makes his way home. He lifts the latch of the garden gate and walks up to the front door. He must have been so distracted this morning that he forgot to put on the alarm when he left the house. In the kitchen, he just sits at the breakfast table, feeling emotional after being fired from his job of twenty years. All alone, he feels like crying.

But just then he hears a thud somewhere in the house. Something must have fallen over. He better investigate. Everything seems the same in the living room. He goes upstairs – all silent. He opens the bedroom door. The sight that confronts him makes him gasp with shock. He stares straight into the startled faces of two people in the room. One is his wife, naked and kneeling on the bed, facing the door. The other is a man in the act of intercourse with the woman, from behind.

"Gordon! What are you doing home?" she cries.

"What's going on? Who's this?" Gordon shouts back.

The naked man gets out of bed and reaches for his clothes. "I'll be off then," he says as he pulls on his boxer shorts.

"Mabel – how could you? How could you do this to me?"

"I can explain," Mabel answers, "he's just a friend."

"That's right mate – just good friends," the interloper says, buttoning his shirt.

"You bastard!" shouts Gordon. He takes a swing at the man but misses, and one punch in return soon knocks him to the floor. He looks up dazed, with his nose bleeding.

"Is that what you wanted? Are you happy now?" Mabel demands.

"Just you behave yourself now," the man tells Gordon. "Me and your missus were just having a bit of fun that's all."

"That's right," agrees Mabel, now less contrite. "He's more fun than you ever were, that's for sure."

"But Mabel…" Gordon can't find the words to say.

"Why don't you just get out and leave us alone. Close the door behind you and don't come back for an hour," Mabel tells him. "He's a real man, not a wimp like you. He gives me a good shagging, which is more than you've ever done."

The man is more confident now and says mockingly "She says you can't even get it up her these days."

"He's never got any money either," adds Mabel." He just babbles on about his old mother and the stupid books he writes."

"Sounds like a bit of a nancy boy if you ask me", remarks the man.

"Oh get him out of here," Mabel tells him, "so we can get back to the fantastic sex we were having".

The man is much heavier than Gordon, and he goes across and lifts him up by his suit jacket lapels. "Come on then, there's a good boy. Don't you know three's a crowd," jokes the man, as he opens the door and throws him out of the bedroom.

"Put that in your next novel," Mabel shouts and the couple laugh at Gordon lying on the carpet. The man shuts the door and Gordon tries to pull himself up. The door opens again. The man throws a copy of Woman's Own down at Gordon.

"Here – read this while you're waiting – maybe there's something on knitting or flower arranging", the man quips and shuts the door again.

Gordon gets to his feet and as he passes the bathroom he takes some toilet paper and wipes the blood from his nose. He tries to ignore the giggling coming from the bedroom, and walks out of the house, humiliated and downcast. He doesn't know where he's going – just anywhere, away from the house, away from his unfaithful wife, away from everything.

Chapter 8

At least I can go for a decent pint of real ale, Gordon thinks as he makes his way to a pub he frequents now and then. It used to be too far from home just to go out for a quiet pint, but now that he has moved into a flat downtown it's only a short walk away. Maybe a couple of pints will cheer him up he hopes, as he opens the door of the Horseshoe Bar. But when there are only a handful of people chatting quietly in the shadows, and the bar's policy is never to play music, it's anything but cheerful. What's happened to pubs these days, goes through his mind as he sips his pint of Bombardier. People just stay in, glued to their tellies and computers. No wonder pubs are so deserted. The pub is full of character with a long horseshoe-shaped mahogany bar and a log fire quietly smouldering. The room itself has an interesting classical look with fine cornicing and two Corinthian pillars.

Time passes and the barman just keeps drying glasses and storing them under the bar. Things look bleak now, Gordon thinks as he finishes off his beer. Better not dwell on it, he advises himself. Better just to get along the road to his one-bedroom rented flat above the kebab takeaway.

He feels the cold air on his face as he walks out of the pub and into the street. Soon be Christmas, but Gordon isn't in much of a mood for rejoicing these days. As he walks home to his flat, he wonders how long his mother would last. He thinks too about losing his job. It wasn't a job he liked particularly, but it kept his head above water, and he liked some of his work mates. But it was the cruel and heartless way his wife had treated him that hurt him most of all. She never had a kind word for him, and never supported his ambition to be a writer of spy fiction.

The streets are quieter now with only the odd person or couple passing by. He notices some figure ahead standing at a bus shelter. As he gets closer he sees it's a woman of a rather striking appearance, not pretty by any means, and not so young either, but wearing a gaudy white vinyl coat, open, and revealing a shocking pink mini-skirt above knee-length boots.

"Looking for a good time tonight?" she says as he approaches. "My flat's just round the corner". He suddenly thinks that this of course is where the city's prostitutes hang out, and it's now on his route home.

"Eh, no – just going home thank you", is his polite reply.

"Aw come on – what harm would it do? Come and have some fun with me", she calls to him.

On he goes leaving the woman standing at the bus shelter. Soon be home - maybe have a glass of rum before bed. In the morning I'll go to see Mum at the hospital.

After a few hundred yards he can make out another solitary figure in the distance, standing in a shop doorway. This time he's prepared for her invitation. As he approaches he glances over at her. She isn't like the other one. This girl is young with long dark hair, maybe Italian or Greek, and Gordon can't help but notice how pretty she is.

"Nights colder now", she says to him in broken English. This is a different approach from the earlier encounter, he thinks as he draws nearer. "It's warm at my place", she continues.

"Just on my way home thanks", Gordon replies.

"What your hurry? Come and spend a little while with me".

Her question makes Gordon stop and consider that he is in no hurry to do anything anymore.

"Where are you from?" he asks her.

She steps forward out of the shadows and into the pale yellow street light. Gordon is surprised that the girl has such a pretty, even beautiful face. She isn't all tarted up like the other one, but is wearing an open black and white dog-tooth coat with a short violet skirt underneath.

"I'm Syrian", is her answer.

"What brings you all the way over here?" Gordon questions.

"Well how about you come on back to my place along the road and I'll tell you about it then".

"Oh no, it's okay thanks – maybe some other time", Gordon quickly replies, deciding not to go any further with the conversation. "Bye now", he adds as he continues on his way.

“Oh don’t go yet – come back a talk a little more. I’ll tell you about my life in Syria”.

Gordon keeps walking without looking back, but he feels there is something impassioned about her last remark. She says no more and goes back to her wretched routine.

Gordon turns the corner and notices the nightclub Cleopatra’s Asp, is getting ready for another late night session of dancing and drinking. A little farther on and he can see Kebabylon at the end of the street. He trudges on and soon he is back in his loathsome accommodation. He turns on the light and scans across his new dwelling. He switches on the old telly and pours the rum he’d promised himself. Now it’s late, and time to sleep at last. But as he sits in front of the decrepit gas fire and sips his rum his thoughts are always the same – how much better it would be if he didn’t wake up in the morning.

Chapter 9

The plane touches down in Manchester at ten in the morning. It's a difficult and inconvenient journey which Gordon has made several times to visit his mother at the Western General Infirmary. How many more times will he make this trip he wonders as the bus leaves the airport for the city. The trees are pretty well bare now, he notices on the way, apart from a few isolated leaves that struggle to hang on.

A taxi takes him from Piccadilly, and finally he arrives at the hospital. At Ward 9 the young nurse comes over to meet him.

"Oh Gordon, nice to see you again. How was your flight?" she asks politely.

"Oh you know, much the same every time. Once in a while would be okay, but every couple of days is tiring", he replies to the young smiling girl.

"Yes it must be hard work to come so frequently", the nurse says, sympathetically.

"Has there been any change?" Gordon enquires.

"No - no change. Much the same really.

"Do you think she'll make it to the weekend?" Gordon asks solemnly.

"Well to be honest, she might linger on for a few days but it's touch and go now".

"Thanks nurse – you've been very understanding throughout this difficult time".

"If I can be of any further help, please let me know". The nurse smiles and turns to walk out of the private ward.

As she walks away Gordon pulls up a chair at the bedside. His mother is not peaceful, and appears agitated. She moves her hand around and stares into space with unseeing eyes. How awful to see his mother so badly brain-damaged that her movements are only random misdirected activity.

Eventually he starts up a monologue, as if really conversing with her.

"So how've you been Mum?" he asks with a cheerful manner. "The leaves are almost all down now. Before you know it, it'll be winter again. Never mind though – at least we can have a nice Christmas together". He reflects for a moment and then continues, "Remember when I was just a little boy, you would've just been a young woman, I used to tell you all my little troubles then. You'd always be there to comfort me when I had tears in my eyes. You'd wipe away my tears and tell me not to cry and everything would be all right again. Well I wish you could comfort me now, because my whole world has imploded overnight. You always told me to be honest with you, and that's what I'd like to do now".

He gets up and goes over to the window. It looks down onto the car park, and cars and taxis are coming and going, and visitors with flowers hurry into the hospital out of the rain. He continues to talk to his mother with his back to her.

"Things just didn't go the way they should have. I've lost my job, my wife and my mother all at once. I've never made anything of my life. I tried writing spy stories, but I've been a failure in everything I've tried to do. There's no hope and no future. I never imagined when I was a teenager that I'd end up with nothing. I should have made the grade by now, but instead I'm just a nobody, and the time has come to put an end to this unbearable life. I've decided that after you've gone, I'll do what I have to do then it's my turn to go".

All is silent as he looks out of the window at the visitors below. He thinks about his life, his mother's imminent death and a dreadfully unhappy future. A lugubrious atmosphere hangs in the private room, as he stares timelessly through the rain spattered window.

"Spend my money!" suddenly shatters the silence. He spins round to face the old lady.

"What did you say? What did you say? Did you say something? Did you say spend your money? Speak to me – what did you say!"

But no words are forthcoming from his mother. She just continues to wave one arm around meaninglessly and stare blindly into space.

"I thought you spoke to me – did you not say 'spend my money'? Did I just imagine it?" He presses her to speak again and again, but she does not respond. Did she speak to him, or was it just his distressed mind playing tricks with him? Gordon sits with his mother for another hour but sees no difference in her vegetative condition. Eventually he gets up and speaks to her before he leaves.

“Okay, I better be going now. Take things easy and just relax and I’ll be back to see you in a couple of days”.

His stomach feels like lead as he slowly walks to the door and looks back at his mother for what might be the last time.

“Bye Mum”, he says quietly, as he turns and walks along the corridor.

Chapter 10

The morning is quiet and peaceful in Zavtak, a fishing village along the Adriatic coast east of Dubrovnik, as Bentley sips a cranberry grappa in a small outdoor café across from the harbour. The gentle lapping of waves and chatter are the only sounds apart from the occasional boat engine starting up as a small craft makes her way across the bay. Behind him some people are enjoying an early lunch, maybe a tuna salad or seafood risotto. Between him and the harbour is a small road, just wide enough for cars, and farther along other cafes are serving beer and coffee. Dressed in a Hawaiian shirt with shorts and sandals, Bentley enjoys the tranquillity of this sleepy Croatian village.

On the other side of the road, an old beige VW Beetle rests forlornly, as if it hasn't seen the open road for twenty years. Just in front of the car, and old man scrapes flaking paint off the bottom of an upturned rowing boat. Bentley sips his grappa, then his espresso. He hears the clip-clop of a horse's hooves. A farmer comes into view leading a chestnut horse along the road by the bridle. As they pass the café where Bentley is sitting, two young children, a boy and a girl, run up to the horse and carefully try to stroke its muzzle. The man who seems to know them, brings two carrots out of his jacket pocket, and gives them one each. The children laugh as they cautiously feed the carrots to the horse. After a minute or two, the children run off and the man and horse continue on their way.

As time passes Bentley gradually becomes aware of the growl of a motorbike in the distance. Fishermen go about their daily work of hauling nets of langoustines from their boats and stacking them on the harbour walls. Bentley sips his grappa again as he looks casually across the bay. The motorbike sound grows louder. The waitress brings out a tray of drinks for the couple behind. The motorbike comes into view. Bentley sits forward. The bike is travelling at speed along the narrow road in front of the row of cafes. There are two on the bike, and both are male. The pillion passenger seems to be carrying something. They are just at the end of the street now, and getting faster. The engine roars as the bike approaches from the left.

The passenger brings something over to his right side. It's a sub-machine gun. Bentley throws himself to the ground as machine gun fire blasts out across the café where he was sitting a moment ago. Bullets ricochet everywhere and smash windows, plates and bottles as the bike hurtles past. People start screaming and running for cover. Bentley escapes injury behind the up-turned table on the café floor.

When the bike has passed he gets to his feet. Gun smoke fills the air and the quiet little street has turned into a state of panic and chaos. Fishermen have returned to the safety of their boats and tourists run frantically about, not knowing which way to go. Bentley looks along to the right. The bike has stopped in the middle of the street, a hundred metres away. The rider manoeuvres the Russian Dnepr back towards the harbour, then forwards, then back again. They're coming back for another attempt to kill him. Bentley sees at the café next to him another motorbike parked at the side of the road. The owner is sitting bolt upright and is staring down the road at the assassins' bike preparing for its second run. Bentley runs over. He sees the keys on the table. "I need your bike," he tells the biker and with those words tips up the table so that the man is thrown backwards and knocked off his chair. He is sent flying across the table behind, and the man and woman there are also knocked backwards as their table collapses and their plates of mussels and calamari go crashing onto the floor.

Bentley jumps onto the Africa Twin trail bike, starts it up and with the front wheel lifted off the road, screams away in the opposite direction. The pair are ready to go again, and with their engine roaring, the chase begins. The two bikes travel along the harbour road at high speed, and Bentley focuses on avoiding people on the road as he flashes by with the pair closing on him behind. He makes a sudden left turn away from the harbour, and up a narrow cobbled street through the village. The assassins follow only metres behind on the Dnepr. Old men dive for cover as the bikes speed along the lanes of the old town. The gunman opens fire again with the machine gun. Bentley tries to keep his head down while swerving from one side to another, while bullets fly everywhere, through cottage windows, into bird cages hanging outside, over the heads of old women who have their lacework on display, indiscriminately blazing through open church doors, ripping up sheets and towels hanging out to dry in the heat of the midday sun.

He turns sharply back down a lane to the left towards the sea, down a long flight of stairs with the killers' bike hot on his tail, and the pillion rider relentlessly firing a barrage of shots from his 9mm Heckler and Koch. People run for their lives as the two bikes career down the old steps towards the harbour, with the thundering sound of gunfire continuing all the way. He can't outrun them - any second now he's a dead man. He swings the Africa Twin round at the foot of the stairs and is back on the main street again where he was sitting quietly just a few minutes before. The killers turn at the bottom of the stairs and they're back on the street, so close the gunman can't miss this time.

The firing stops. Bentley looks in the mirror. The pillion rider has removed the curved magazine from the MP5 machine gun. He is out of ammunition and needs to reload. The street is wider and both bikes accelerate with only ten metres between them. Bentley knows he must find a way out of this before the gunman attaches another magazine or he's dead for sure.

Some distance away a bunch of black cables are draped lazily across the road about four metres high carrying power to the boats berthed in the harbour. Bentley carefully lifts himself up so that his left foot can reach the saddle. The street is full of the deafening roar of the bikes and the smell of gunpowder and exhaust fumes. Now both feet are on the seat. He is crouching on the bike but still holding the handlebars. Trays of jewellery are sent flying as local craftswomen dive out of the path of the oncoming bikes. The Dnepr is closing on him. He puts his right foot on the throttle and then releases his left hand. Mouths agape, astounded onlookers are held in suspended animation as the bikes flash past. His left foot is on the tank and his right is keeping the bike steady while locked at full throttle. He struggles to keep control of the Africa Twin with the full force of the wind against him. The gunman clicks the magazine into position. Now both Bentley's hands are free. He approaches the cables and when directly under them springs up to grab the black wires, which are pulled downwards with his weight. The momentum of the bike drives his legs forwards and right round in a single circular movement. As he come swinging back round, the assailants' bike is passing underneath and in one continuous move both feet hit the gunman right between the shoulders. The passenger lurches violently into the driver who immediately loses control of the machine. The bike speeds across the street, and the front wheel hits the upturned rowing boat. The bike is impelled onto the bonnet of the Beetle, across the roof and catapulted over the harbour wall. Time stands still as the assailants soar over the bay and are flung into the sea as the bike crashes onto the deck of a passing fishing boat.

Bentley's drops down onto the street and walks across to the scene in the harbour. People have crowded round to look at the pair thrashing around in the water. He joins the crowd and to an old local woman who clearly doesn't understand, remarks "I hope they don't harbour a grudge", and with a wry smirk slips quietly away. Along the street he passes the Africa Twin which has come to rest safely on a heap of sacks of grain. With a sharp tug, it's back on the centre stand.

Gordon sighs as the plane touches down at Manchester airport. Once again a rainy day. This might very well be the last time he visits the city. Today he is smartly dressed – grey suit, white shirt, black tie. He won't be going to the hospital today. This time it's to his mother's funeral.

Chapter 11

Night falls over the city and Gordon can't seem to focus on anything at the moment. He can smell the greasy fast food from Kebabylon downstairs as he watches people coming and going from his window. Must be months now, he reflects, since he ended up in this God-awful hovel. On his table lie a few electronic parts, switches, transistors, resistors, next to a soldering iron. He paces restlessly, flicks from channel to channel, but nothing of interest. Finally he throws on his jacket and heads out to the Horseshoe Bar for a pint or two. There's not much to keep him in these days, and maybe a couple of drinks will cheer him up. At least it's a better pub than the Anal Bar on Switchback Road he sometimes had a drink in on his way home to Bearsden. He wonders if the C had ever been replaced on the sign above the door after it fell off some years ago. The streets are ablaze with a rainbow of fiery colours from the neon lights of bars and cafes, and relentlessly changing traffic lights along the way.

Along the road he passes the black exterior of The Gravy Yard, the world's first zombie restaurant. He could imagine the white-faced waiter saying to some curious couple, "On the menu we have Breast of Peasant, Mariner's Muscles, and tonight's special is Hungarian Ghoulish."

On he trudges, head bowed, wondering how come things turned out this way. A short distance away he notices a figure sheltering at a bus stop. As he gets closer he sees it's a girl. Now it dawns on him – this is the girl who tried to persuade him to go back to her flat last time he walked along this street. This must be her patch. As he walks past the girl he raises his head to look at her.

"Do you have a light?" she asks him as he passes.

"I'm sorry I don't smoke", is Gordon's reply.

"Neither do I".

Her surprise reply causes him to stop in front of her momentarily before continuing.

"I know you", she calls as he turned his back on her to walk away. "You walked past here a few days ago".

"I walk here when I go out for a drink," he says as he continues on his way.

"Don't you like me?" she suddenly asks.

Gordon stops for a minute and politely replies, "Of course I do but I don't know you".

"Why not get to know me?"

He is dumbfounded for a moment. She stands in the middle of the pavement looking at him in a strangely imploring way, and as before he can't help but notice how pretty she is. He finds himself searching for a reason why he shouldn't speak to her.

"You don't seem like the other women who hang around here".

"My flat's just along the road. Please come round until the rain stops".

She slowly starts to walk across the road, looking back to see if Gordon will follow.

"What do you have to lose?" goes through his mind as he begins to walk in her direction. They walk a few metres apart in silence as she takes him back to her tenement flat. On the corner they pass a chip shop pretentiously named 'The Squid Squad', although it probably never sold squid.

It's a run-down, dingy top floor flat she takes him to. Yellowing white paint is flaking off the close walls as they walk up the stairs to her front door. Inside, a seedy sight greets his eyes. It's a one room flat in a poor state of decoration, and it looks like it hasn't seen a lick of paint in years.

The room has a double bed, old gas cooker, sink, table, two chairs. A bare light bulb hangs overhead, and a dirty white sheet is draped across the window. Wall paper is peeling from the walls, and there's an unpleasant musty smell in the room. She takes off her coat, then sits on the dirty duvet and starts to take off her boots.

"Do you own the flat?" Gordon asks.

"I don't live here. They own it. I just work here."

"Who are *they*?" he enquires.

"The men I work for. The men who brought me here", she replies and starts to remove her skirt.

"Now hold on just a minute – I'm not in the mood for that just now", he tells her.

"You don't want sex? I thought that's why you came here"

Gordon sighs. "I've got something on my mind at the moment."

"But if they saw you come in and you don't pay me, I'll get into trouble".

Gordon takes two twenties out of his wallet. "Is that enough?"

She puts the money in her purse, and pulls up her skirt again.

"Come over here – sit down for a minute", he suggests.

"Better not be too long. What is it that you want?" she asks.

Gordon sits pensively for a moment or two.

"You know, sometimes you look around and there's not a single person to talk to – not your family, not your friends, nobody. You don't know me and you couldn't care what happens to me, could you?"

She just sits quietly and Gordon's unfortunate story begins to unfold.

"I was made redundant, caught my wife in bed with another man and my mother died, all within the space of a couple of weeks."

"That's too bad. I'm sorry to hear that", she responds politely.

"I'm at the end of my tether now. My mother told me before she died to spend her savings, but what's the point? That wouldn't solve anything. Everything's turned so sour that I just feel like going back to my rented flat, putting a rope around my neck and hanging myself from the gas meter on the kitchen wall."

"How much did your mother leave you?" she asks.

"A hundred grand", is Gordon's reply.

She gives a quick up-and-down whistle. "What you could do with a hundred grand".

"What *could* I do with a hundred grand?" questions Gordon. "Spend a year in the Caribbean? Go round the world on my own? Buy a new car? What would be the point of that? It wouldn't make me any happier. I've considered giving it to charity before I make an appointment with the gas meter".

"Is that what your mum would have wanted – to struggle all her life just so you can give it all away just to get rid of it? If she'd wanted that she could have done it herself".

Gordon is taken aback by her candour.

"Well if I don't find a good use for that money soon, I'll be standing on that lonely ladder, and the money'll go to my wife".

“There must be something you’ve always really wanted to do? Some dream or ambition?” she asks.

“The only ambition I’ve ever had was to be a writer of secret agent novels, but I never got any of them published. I was just a failure”.

“Can’t you find a way to promote them with your mother’s money?”

“Nobody’d be interested in them. It’s too late to do anything with them now. They just weren’t a success. I wish I’d done things differently but my whole life’s just been a waste of time”.

“Is there no one you admire?” she asks. “Someone you could be like?”

Gordon smiles for a moment. “Well there is someone I wish I were like - John Bentley”.

“Who’s John Bentley?” she asks.

“John Bentley is my fictitious hero, who lives in a world of glamour and danger. He is surrounded by beautiful women, drives supercars, speaks seven languages and is a secret agent for British Intelligence.”

“Well why can’t you be John Bentley for a while, and use some of the money to pay for a lifestyle like his?”

“How could I live a life like his?” Gordon asks.

“What if you spent some of that money on going on the kind of adventure that you wrote for your hero? You could live out the part for a while, until you run out of money, and then who knows what you’ll do after that – hang yourself if you want, or spend the rest of your life living cheaply somewhere on some South Sea island in the Pacific. Maybe it’ll make you a better writer and you won’t want to kill yourself after all”.

Suddenly someone is banging on the door. “Are you in there? Come on, let’s go. There’s a man downstairs waiting to come up!” a man shouts from outside.

“All right I’m coming”, she shouts back.

“Who’s that?” Gordon asks.

“That’s the guy who runs this place. You better go – you’ve been here too long”, she says under her breath.

“Hurry up! Are you ready?” shouts the man at the door.

“Just coming”, she shouts back.

Gordon gets to his feet and goes over to the door. She straightens herself and opens the front door, and Gordon leaves the flat. The fat, bald man with a gold chain round his neck, dirty shirt hanging out and sweaty smell steps aside as Gordon walks past. On the stairs he passes a middle-aged man in a raincoat going up to visit her. They exchange unfriendly glances as they pass one another. Gordon hears a few quietly-spoken words on the landing, then the closing of the door.

Chapter 12

Mr Grimshaw sits behind his desk in the solicitor's office just along from Central Station. On his desk are folders full of documents. He is dressed in a sober grey suit, white shirt and dark tie. There are no pictures on the walls – just a calendar. He is talking to his secretary on the phone.

"Oh thanks Nancy – show him in please".

Nancy opens the door and allows Gordon to walk into Grimshaw's office.

"Ah Gordon, do come in", Grimshaw says as he offers his hand to Gordon. "Please have a seat."

Gordon sits across the desk from Grimshaw. He has been asked to attend this meeting with the family solicitor of Mabel and Gordon.

"Firstly I'd like to begin by offering my sincere condolences on the passing away of your mother".

"Thank you," replies Gordon quietly.

"It must be a very difficult time for you just now. I heard that you were also made redundant from the shipping job".

"Yes, I'm afraid so".

Grimshaw's tone becomes more serious as he continues.

"You'll have heard by now of your wife's intention to file for divorce".

"Yes I heard", replies Gordon.

"Well I'll come straight to the point. Your wife intends to divorce you on the grounds of adultery, and sue you for two thirds of your estate, including your savings and the marital home".

Gordon is visibly shaken by this news.

"She's accusing *me* of adultery! She's the one guilty of adultery!" Gordon declares.

"Do you have any witnesses to support your allegation?" Grimshaw asks.

"Yeah the bastard I caught her in bed with", answers Gordon.

"Well he isn't likely to corroborate your story, is he?"

Grimshaw pauses for a moment, and then adds a new twist to the regrettable saga.

“Gordon, I have to bring it to your attention that on Wednesday night on the 17th of this month, you were seen walking into the premises of a prostitute known to the police. You were inside the premises known as a brothel to the police for a period of twenty five minutes. You were then seen leaving the premises at ten fifteen that evening. Please look at these photographs”.

Grimshaw hands photographs to Gordon of him entering and leaving the flat. Stunned by this development Gordon tries to protest his innocence.

“But I only went to her flat to talk to her. No sex took place!”

“If you say so, but in a court of law it would appear highly unlikely that you went to a brothel with a prostitute only for the purpose of conversation. The photographs are all the evidence your wife will need to sue you for adultery”

“How did you get these photographs?” Gordon asks.

“Your wife employed a private detective to follow your movements, in the hope she could find something to pin on you. It looks like you handed it to her on a silver platter”, Grimshaw explains.

“Oh my God – this can’t be happening! I’ve done nothing wrong”. Gordon is suddenly chilled by another thought.

“What about the inheritance my mother left me?”

“I’m afraid your wife would be entitled to two thirds of that too”

With mouth half-closed Gordon mutters to himself, “So the bitch wants to take me to the cleaners”.

Chapter 13

The neon sign above Kebabylon casts a lurid glow into Gordon's rooms. All is quiet apart from the occasional sound of traffic below. A pervasive atmosphere of gloom dwells in his depressing flat. The only enjoyment he will expect this evening is a couple of pints somewhere later on. For the time being he sits at his computer, calling up some information from the internet. On the screen there are diagrams of automatic pistols and magazines with some accompanying text. One is entitled 'How to build a working firearm'.

An hour goes by until he shuts down the computer, gets his coat, scarf and gloves and heads out for the couple of pints he promised himself.

No girl at the bus stop tonight as he makes his way to the pub. It's cold now that winter's arrived. He wonders if she's round at her place, maybe with some sleazy client. His pace slows as he starts to consider wandering round there. Maybe not a good idea – let's just get along to the pub. But then he begins to head towards her flat. He passes the Squid Squad on the corner and stands across the road from the tenement. All in darkness – no one to be seen anywhere. He cautiously walks into the close and up the stairs. No sign of the fat man with the gold chain and sweaty smell. He silently creeps up the stairs until he's on the landing at the top. Some faint music inside the room. For a moment he stands motionless, and finally plucks up the courage to knock quietly on the door. When the door opens the girl's expression changes from surprise as her face seems to momentarily light up at the sight of Gordon.

"Hello," he whispers. "I was just passing and I thought I might speak to you for a minute."

She opens the door with a vague smile. Thankfully she is alone as Gordon walks inside. They sit together by the one-bar fire on two old wooden chairs.

"Are we having sex this time?" she asks.

"No, not now. I just came to say that I'm leaving tomorrow to go on my secret agent adventure. It was your idea to go, so I came to say goodbye".

For a moment her face betrays a sense of sadness at his news.

"I don't know how it will go, or where I'll end up, but if I stay here, there's no telling what I'll end up doing."

"Well that's good news – at least you can spend your mother's money before your wife gets her hands on it", she replies.

A pause in the faltering conversation directs Gordon's attention to some music which is quietly playing.

"What is that music?" he asks. "It's tango music, isn't it?"

"Yes – it reminds me of back in my home country", she replies pensively.

"But you're not Spanish – where did you say you were from again?"

"I'm from Syria. My father used to teach me tango when we lived there."

"What brought you to Glasgow?" Gordon asks.

"Our family had to flee from Aleppo when the civil war started. We tried to make a new life away from the war-torn country".

"So this is your new life?"

"This is my life from now on", she replies with a sigh of resignation.

"But what about your family – what happened to them?"

After what seemed to be an interminable pause, she eventually answers his question.

"We lived in a village a few kilometres outside Aleppo. We awoke to hear the rumble of engines and rattle and squeak of tracks as Government tanks rolled out of the mist as dawn was breaking. My father grabbed me from my bed and my mother picked up my younger sister and only wearing coats and pyjamas we ran for shelter under a stone bridge over the small frozen river. The tanks began shelling the village. All we could do was watch in horror as one by one the houses were blown apart. Our house was hit and soon it was ablaze. In minutes it was razed to the ground. We were happy in that house for many years. I used to play with my sister in the garden. I learnt to play the piano there.

After the tanks had destroyed the village we hurried away from the bridge and joined other refugees who were running from the column of tanks. My father looted some burnt-out houses along the way to try and find some food and warm clothing for the family. He found some money and jewellery – wedding rings, necklaces, watches.

We walked for miles through the night and we came upon an abandoned car at the side of the road. It was riddled with bullet holes and there was blood on the seats but my father managed to get it started. We'd heard from some of the refugees that the road to Latakia was clear so all the next day we drove down to the coast. Along the way we saw lines of ragged refugees, but my father kept driving at speed without stopping for anything. It was a miracle that the soldiers we saw on the road didn't pull us over. I remember in the car that it was warm and for a moment we felt a sense of relief that we were fleeing from danger".

She suddenly becomes aware that she had spoken at length as she relived her disturbing story. "I shouldn't have said so much".

"No, no," Gordon quickly answers. "Please carry on".

After a moment's deliberation, she continues her harrowing story.

"When we finally got to Latakia there were thousands of people all massing around the docks trying to find a boat to take them away from Syria. The whole quayside was in a state of panic. My father searched along the seafront and shouted to us to run over. He'd found a cargo ship that was ready to leave for Brindisi in the south of Italy in a few minutes. He had to pay all the money and jewellery he had to get us on the ship. There was a huge desperate crowd on the harbour all trying to get aboard. We tried to keep together but the crowd was so big and so frantic that my father and I got on board but my mother and sister were pushed aside and we became separated with my father and I forced below the deck of the cargo ship. My mother and sister must have been left behind on the dock. That was the last I ever saw of them.

The crossing to Brindisi was very difficult. People were sick and some were wailing, and it was so overcrowded and stifling we couldn't breathe. There was no food or water for the whole passage. We were kept in the hold and told to keep quiet or we'd be thrown overboard. It seemed to last forever, but eventually we sailed into Brindisi at night and were ordered off the ship and into the darkness.

My father said he had a friend in Naples who would help us, so we began a long journey across Italy. At a petrol station on the road to Naples we saw a covered lorry which was registered in Naples and we managed to climb into the back while the driver was in the café.

We were starving but at least there was some hope that we would reach Naples and my father's friend would take us in and look after us. The drive was rough and uncomfortable but we could relax for a while in the back of the lorry. I kept thinking about what had happened to my mother and sister and picturing their faces when we were separated on the quayside."

Again she sits back and becomes silent, either because the awful experience is too upsetting, or perhaps because she feels she shouldn't talk so openly to a stranger.

"What happened after that?" asks Gordon.

Again she appears to wander into a trance as she recalls the events of that tortuous journey.

"Half way to Naples my father took seriously ill. Maybe it was the sight of the house burning down, or the dreadful experience crossing the Mediterranean, or losing my mother and sister, but he suffered a heart attack and died under the canvas cover of the truck to Naples. I held his hand as he drew his last few breaths, and stroked his face, and then he silently passed away as the lorry continued along the highway. Six hours or so passed as I sat beside him until I felt the truck slowing down. We were approaching the outskirts of the city. At a level crossing, I crawled out from the back and quietly slipped away. I had no choice but to leave my father on the truck.

I didn't know how to get in touch with my father's friend, so I ended up sleeping rough with some gypsies, and stayed alive by stealing food from shops and money from people's pockets. A year went by until one day some man offered to take me to London where he said I'd be able to work as a nanny. I was destitute in Naples, so I agreed, and he somehow managed to smuggle me all the way across Europe until we took a boat at night across the English Channel.

When I got to London, there was no job as a nanny. I ended up in Glasgow and I was forced to be a prostitute. I had no passport, no money and nowhere to live, so that's how come I came to be in Glasgow".

"But that's a really terrible story – is there nothing you can do to help yourself?" Gordon asks with a sense of desperation.

"Every time I hear someone knock on that door, some dirty creep who makes me have sex with him, I ask myself that question, and when he leaves, I play my tango music and remember dancing with my father".

Suddenly someone bangs on the door.

"How long are you gonna be in there? There's a guy waiting for you here."

She jumps up. "I'll be right there – give me a minute!"

"You better go", she tells Gordon.

Gordon gets up to go. "My name's Gordon. What's yours?"

"I'm Zoulla. I must go now".

Gordon leaves the room, passes the fat man on the landing and walks down the stairs and into the night.

Chapter 14

Monte Carlo casino has a relaxed atmosphere, yet with a quiet undercurrent of excitement. There is a murmur of voices and rattle of bouncing roulette balls in the exclusive 19th century gambling hall. Spectacular chandeliers and exquisite baroque walls and ceilings give a unique ambience of wealth and class inside the legendary building. Ladies displaying necklaces with diamonds, sapphires and other expensive jewellery enter on the arms of men in impeccable black dinner suits as they prepare for an evening's entertainment at the casino.

"Place your bets, ladies and gentlemen", invites the croupier to the group around the roulette wheel. Bentley, who is smartly dressed in a white dinner jacket and black bow tie pushes forward a stack of chips. Beside him is an attractive young woman wearing a purple satin evening dress with a plunging neckline that reveals much of her cleavage. She has a voluptuous figure with curvaceous bust and hips, and her long blond hair falls down over her shoulders.

The croupier spins the wheel and enters the ball in the opposite direction. All eyes follow the wheel and watch anxiously to see which pocket the ball will ultimately select. Once again it wasn't in Bentley's favour.

"You're new here, aren't you?" the girl asks him.

"Yes I am", he replies politely.

"You don't seem to be having much luck tonight".

"Well money's for burning, isn't it", he answers with an air of nonchalance.

"Let me introduce myself. I'm Desiree", she tells him.

"John Bentley. Enchanted to meet you".

In an office somewhere upstairs two men in suits and ties are watching Bentley and the girl, and listening in on their conversation. They sit in front of a wall of monitors which relate information about the unsuspecting clients in the gambling hall. They have singled out Bentley for special attention.

"Who *is* that guy?" one man asks. "He's never been here before but he's spending money like there was no tomorrow. The doorman tells me he arrived in a Maserati."

"There's something suspicious about him. Look how serious he is – he never smiles and look at the bulge under his left arm. I think he's wearing a shoulder holster."

"He's been here every night this week, losing a fortune as if he's waiting for something to happen."

"Could it be he's the new British agent? The last one was murdered a month ago."

"Maybe we should let the boss know, just in case."

"Better keep him here – let him win for a while."

This time Bentley gathers in a pile of chips with both hands.

"Well Mr Bentley, your luck seems to be changing", Desiree notices.

"Win or lose, makes no difference to me," is his answer.

"What brings you to Monte Carlo?" she asks.

"I'm on business for the British Government."

The man in front of the monitor looks up at the other.

"What did I tell you? I knew he was the replacement agent."

Once again Bentley pulls a large pile of chips towards him.

"Looks like you're on a winning streak now!" says the girl excitedly.

"Well – easy come, easy go", is his casual reply as he passes the large pile of chips towards her. "Why don't you cash these in and buy yourself something nice?"

"There must be five thousand dollars' worth there! You'd give that to a total stranger?"

"Why not?"

He thanks the group with whom he was playing and bids them goodnight.

"Why don't we go back to your hotel room?" she asks." We can get a bottle of Moet and Chandon and celebrate our good fortune.

"Keep away from the 2003", he warns her. "It was a very poor year".

They collect their coats from the cloakroom and make their way towards the front door. The air is cool as they leave the casino.

"Let's get a cab", Desiree suggests. "Which hotel are you staying in?"

"I'm at the International", he replies. "What brings you to Monte Carlo?"

"Oh I came with some friends, but they've gone home now", she answers.

A taxi is waiting at the entrance to the casino, and they casually stroll across to it. Suddenly a man appears out of the shadows, comes up behind Bentley and stabs a syringe into the side of his neck. Bentley reels and starts to lose consciousness as the door is opened and he is bundled into the back of the taxi.

"Good work Desiree", the man says as he gets into the taxi. He pulls the door shut and the taxi speeds away.

Chapter 15

A middle-aged man in a light blue linen suit sits behind a large mahogany desk reading today's Le Monde. To his right a younger black man in a smart grey suit pours coffee and brings a cup over to the man at the desk. The window behind the desk looks out onto the aquamarine serenity of the Mediterranean.

A buzzer sounds on the desk, and the man responds by pressing the talk switch on the panel.

"Monsieur, pourriez-vous s'il vous plaît le voir maintenant?" the telephonic voice asks through the intercom.

"Ah oui – je le voir tout de suite. Amenez-le au bureau, s'il vous plaît," the man answers.

He sips his coffee as the younger man tidies cups and saucers at the drinks cabinet by the office wall. A moment later the door opens. A man reverses in pulling what for a moment looks like a delivery trolley. It is in fact a wheelchair carrying a man with a black satin cummerbund over his eyes. His wrists are tied to the armrests of the wheelchair. He is swung round into a position of facing the man behind the desk. The blindfold is removed – it is Bentley. He squints at the light and blinks several times.

"Ah, Mr Bentley", the man begins. "I must apologise for the less than courteous manner by which I brought you here".

Bentley peers at his silhouette against the shimmer of the sea outside. An instruction is given to the manservant.

"Conrad - fermez les volets, s'il vous plaît".

The manservant comes over and closes the shutters behind the desk. A ceiling fan whirrs quietly overhead. The man who brought him in unties his wrists, and leaves the office.

"So this is your office. Nice view of the sea," Bentley remarks.

"Café pour Monsieur Bentley, Conrad."

"Oui, Monsieur Lafarge," the manservant replies.

"I invited you here today to answer a few questions. What brings you to Monte Carlo?"

"A spot of sea fishing", is Bentley's flippant reply.

"And what about this?" He opens a drawer and pulls out a handgun. "You were wearing this pistol. Why would you be carrying a gun?"

"I thought I'd have a go at clay pigeon shooting".

The manservant hands a cup of coffee to Bentley and leaves the room.

"This gun of yours – very interesting. It's made of plastic like an imitation gun, yet it's capable of firing live ammunition. Easy to smuggle through customs, and looks like a child's toy, yet very much a real weapon. Very clever. Now perhaps you'd like to tell me what you're doing here".

"The British Government has sent me here to find you and help you with your organisation", Bentley replies earnestly.

The man behind the desk laughs. "You found *us*? Very amusing – you found *us*!"

"It worked didn't it?" replies Bentley.

"So why would you want to find us and in what way could you help our organisation?" he enquires.

"British Intelligence has had you under surveillance for some time now. They know what you're up to".

"And what *are* we up to, Mr Bentley?"

"Come on Lafarge – are we going to go round in circles all day? The British Government didn't send me here just to play games with you. If you want our help you better start communicating a lot better than you're doing now. You better start giving me some decent information about your outfit or you'll get into something that you can't possibly understand", Bentley warns him.

"Well why don't we start with you telling me exactly what you know about us", Lafarge suggests.

"I think you've got things the wrong way round Lafarge" begins Bentley. "If we didn't already know about you I wouldn't be sitting here now. We know what you're planning and I think you better start telling me about it."

"I don't really think you're in a position to make demands of *me*, Mr Bentley", remarks Lafarge irksomely.

"If you know what's good for you, you'll come straight to the point", advises Bentley.

Lafarge gets up from his green leather armchair and goes over to the table from where Conrad had been serving coffee. He pours himself another without speaking, as if deep in thought about Bentley's remarks. He slowly stirs the coffee before returning to the chair.

"So Mr Bentley – you're referring to Marrakesh?" he finally asks.

"Of course I'm referring to Marrakesh. Why else would I be here?" Bentley replies.

"And therefore you also know about the President's state visit?"

"Of course - MI6 is already aware of your operation. We're prepared to offer you help if we can".

"Why would MI6 have any interest in the President of the DRC?"

It takes Bentley a moment before he gives his answer.

"MI6 has had agents in the DRC for many years observing its political situation".

"The DRC is a desperately poor third world country. What benefit would it have for Britain?" Lafarge enquires.

Bentley sits back in his chair and carefully considers his answer before replying.

"Not only does the Democratic Republic of Congo have unlimited reserves of gold and copper, our intelligence tells us there are vast underground oil fields which so far lie undiscovered. Britain would like to set up drilling operations in the country".

"And what's that got to do with the President of the DRC?" Lafarge asks.

"We know the situation with the President – we just want to co-ordinate a few things with you first to be sure it'll be worth our while getting involved", replies Bentley.

"You mean what happens after the assassination?" answers Lafarge.

Again Bentley responds after some deliberation.

"The existing President would not consider having British companies drilling for oil on DRC sovereign territory, but with him out of the way, the British Government could make billions of dollars in oil revenue, and support the new regime so we could keep our activities in oil going for many years to come".

Lafarge nods slowly as he tries to absorb Bentley's proposals.

“Why would an organised crime ring like yours take on the assassination of an African president if it weren’t because you also want regime change?” Bentley continues. “We both want the same thing and that’s why I’m here. The British Government wants to set up a new administration in the DRC but we need an outside agency to do it which has substantial knowledge of the personnel involved. In short, we want the new President to be the right man for the job.”

“And how does our organisation benefit from helping you?”

“Your organisation would operate within the new government to keep the president in office. Not only would you be paid very well, you’d become a respectable department keeping up surveillance and reporting any indications of political unrest to our agents. Once in office your underworld would have a free and legitimate hand in any form of business enterprise you chose to establish, and with the undercover support of the British Government”.

Conrad comes back into the room and takes away Bentley’s empty cup, as Lafarge sits back in his chair, pensively stroking his chin as he considers Bentley’s proposal. After Conrad has left he leans forward.

“If what you say is true, then I’d like you to do something to convince me that your intentions are genuine. It’s just a little test and if you pass I’ll accept your plan”, he tells Bentley.

“What do you have in mind”, Bentley enquires.

“I want you to kill the President on Friday”.

“Me kill the President? Don’t you have a marksman arranged?”

“Of course we do – but I want you to prove that what you’re saying is true.”

“What are the details of the assassination?” asks Bentley.

“The President will be in Marrakesh on Friday. He will be arriving at the Hotel Touareg at twelve o’clock for lunch. You will be waiting for him at the top of the clock tower across the square armed with a high velocity rifle with a telescopic viewfinder. When he leaves the hotel and goes towards his limousine you will shoot him through the head and make your escape down the stairs and into the street where you will disappear into the crowd. One hour later you will buy a drink at the Café Moussa where one of our men will be waiting for you. If you succeed I’ll do business with you. If you fail you’re a dead man.”

"You haven't told me yet why you want him shot", Bentley asks.

"You were right - like you we want a regime change so a new President will look favourably on our interests in the DRC".

"What interest are those?" asks Bentley, "Copper mining?"

"Not copper, Mr Bentley – diamonds".

Chapter 16

The old town of Marrakesh has a peculiar historic charm, vibrant with the sound of curious musical instruments, the rattle of step-through motor bike engines, and traders in the old bazaar shouting across the stalls of fish and vegetables and sundry goods at one another. The market is a blaze of colour with the most unusual and exotic fruit on display, and the splendour of a thousand kinds of flowers fills the air with a fragrant, mysterious scent.

Dressed casually in an off-white linen suit and Panama hat, Bentley wanders through the market, glancing down at open sacks of herbs and spices, as vendors call at him, trying to inveigle him into visiting their stalls. The narrow indoor alleys are alive with the bustling throng of people, jostling and pushing their way through the crowded bazaar.

With some effort he manages to struggle to one of the doors to the street. A teenage boy passes, guiding a pair of goats. Outside he looks up, and across the square is the old clock tower from which he is to take up his position as a sniper tomorrow. He glances around; he checks the buildings on either side, and their exits and lanes leading away from the square. Having familiarised himself with the clock tower and surrounding area, he walks away from the square and along one of the ancient streets of the Touareg district.

Time passes from day to evening as he strolls along the narrow cobbled lanes, stopping to observe the Moorish architecture of the city and the unique ethnic character of Marrakesh. Twilight starts to descend over the city as Bentley eventually decides to stop at a traditional Moroccan restaurant for dinner. Inside the atmosphere is busy and overhead fans quietly cool the sultry air. A veil of smoke from the hookah pipes which men are smoking adds a strong essence of Arabic tobacco to the ambience of the restaurant.

He is shown to an alcove table by a waiter and asks for a glass of chai as he settles at the table. It is a dimly-lit and noisy room with local customers talking loudly with each other, and the harsh music of a strange wind instrument is playing somewhere in the background. When the waiter arrives with the tea, Bentley states his order of lamb couscous and a glass of coconut water. He thinks about his mission tomorrow and wonders if it will all go as expected. He looks at people around the restaurant; nothing out of the ordinary, he thinks as he sips the chai.

Suddenly a black African man rushes forward and sits on Bentley's right side in the alcove. Before Bentley has had time to compose himself after the surprise intrusion, the man bursts forth with an excited barrage of words.

"You must not kill the President tomorrow! Do not interfere with matters you do not understand!"

It dawns on Bentley where he has seen the man before. It is Conrad – Lafarge's manservant.

"What are you doing here?" he asks Conrad.

"I've come to implore you – if you assassinate President Marengo it will cause a civil war in the country. Thousands will die of bloodshed, starvation and disease. He is a good man – he is trying to bring peace to the DRC after hundreds of years of conflict and chaos. Lafarge only seeks to create a puppet government so his organisation can plunder the country's resources. He doesn't care about the poor people who struggle to survive!"

Through the cacophony of music and chatter three dull, muffled thuds are heard and Conrad falls forward into Bentley's arms. He has been shot at close range in the back. As Bentley supports the dying man he looks around for the assailant, but none is seen.

"Don't kill the President", Conrad whispers faintly as his breathing becomes shallow and irregular. His head bows forward abruptly, and Bentley carefully rests him against the curved back of the alcove seat. He looks around – no one seems to have noticed. Before the waiter returns with the meal, Bentley leaves a handful of coins on the table, and quietly walks towards the front door and out into the street.

Chapter 17

Friday arrives and Bentley has breakfast at the hotel. His choice is always salubrious; no cooked breakfast but instead grapefruit, muesli, croissant and coffee. Today is an important day and nothing must go wrong. Overnight he considered Conrad's plea, and what he had tried to tell him. Dressed and ready to go, Bentley leaves the hotel, and makes his way to the old town square.

It is just after eight o'clock as he reaches the clock tower. He looks around from across the street. A man leads a donkey laden with multi-coloured rolls of fabric. Some people are setting up stalls and others are going to work, but nothing seems suspicious. He stands with his back against the Touareg Hotel where President Marengo will arrive at twelve o'clock and looks up at the window from where he will aim the rifle. The hands of the clock read twenty to four. They haven't moved for years.

After some time has passed he notices a man carrying an attaché case approaching the clock tower. The man of local appearance and dressed in brown overalls, opens the door of the tower and goes inside. Fifteen minutes later the door opens and he leaves without the case.

Time wears on as Bentley looks for any activity in the street. All continues to appear normal, as he sips a Turkish coffee from outside a café next to the hotel. When eleven thirty arrives, he casually pays the waiter and walks slowly out of the café.

Looking around, he opens the door to the clock tower. Inside is a spiral staircase. He begins to climb the creaking wooden stairs. It's a long walk to the top and his footsteps kick up dust which dances in the rays of sunlight from the old tower's broken windows. He reaches the landing at the top of the staircase and the rusty hinges of the heavy wooden door produce a loud creaking sound as he enters the room. The old broken workings of the clock hang silently above his head, and below is a tiny window. And there, on a stand on the floor is the AK47 assault rifle which he will use to assassinate President Marengo.

He takes off his jacket and hangs it on a nail on the wall. It is hot and stuffy inside the tower. From the window he has a perfect vantage point of the hotel entrance below. Quarter to twelve. He sits on the wooden stool and lifts the rifle from its stand and checks it over. The magazine and telescopic sights are attached. Through the viewfinder he can clearly see where the President will be walking towards him when he leaves the hotel after lunch and goes back to the limo. Everything is now ready – he just needs to wait for the President to arrive. Minutes tick away and small beads of sweat form on Bentley's forehead.

Twelve o'clock and dead on time the black presidential car appears along the street and heads towards the hotel. There are two police motorcycles in front and another state car behind the President's extended Mercedes. The motorcade gets closer until the vehicles draw up in front of the hotel and come to a halt at the entrance. A small reception committee is waiting on the red carpet in front of the hotel. An official from the car behind comes over to the President's car and opens the back door. At last, the president steps out of the car. Now all Bentley has to do is to wait for an hour or so in the stuffy clock tower for the President to leave the hotel. An hour passes. The chauffeur waits inside the limousine, and the motorcycle police stand by their bikes. The second car waits behind. On each side of the doorway two stone monumental lions decorate the entrance. The heat becomes intense in the tower, as Bentley waits for the moment of action. Some activity stirs at the door of the hotel. The President is ready to leave. Bentley lifts the Kalashnikov. The butt of the rifle is now in position on Bentley's shoulder with his eye to the telescopic sight and his finger on the trigger.

The President is now in the perfect position for Bentley to fire. Through the viewfinder Bentley places the cross-hairs directly on Marengo's forehead as he leaves the hotel entrance. From this range he can't miss. His finger slowly squeezes the trigger. The President will be obscured by the group in a few seconds. Bentley sits still and holds the rifle on the stand. The cross-hairs are exactly positioned on Marengo's head. He pulls the trigger and one shot roars out. The bullet shatters the windscreen of the President's car. The people below are momentarily stunned by the explosion of the windscreen. Bentley fires again and a second blast is heard. One of the stone lions' heads is blown into a million fragments. Now the President's aides and the welcoming party realise that an assassination attempt is in progress. The President is hurried into the hotel by his assistants and the group scatter in every direction. The men from the car behind are crouching outside the car and pointing pistols at nearby buildings. Bentley fires again. The plate-glass window of the hotel foyer is destroyed by the third bullet with a deafening crash. The President has managed to escape unharmed inside the hotel and the police escort start checking all nearby buildings to find the sniper.

Bentley leaves the rifle on the stand, grabs his jacket and runs down the wooden spiral staircase as fast as possible. Outside he can hear sirens and people screaming as he makes his escape from the clock tower. He runs down towards the bottom of the tower. The door is in front of him, but no one is there. Get out, get out, get out, he gasps as he approaches the door. He throws the door open – no one there. He runs out into the street. A silver BMW screeches to a halt right in front of him and two men leap out. A few seconds later Bentley is forced into the back of the car. The driver hits the gas and the BMW accelerates away at speed.

Chapter 18

A virtuoso performance of Chopin's Nocturnes can be heard throughout the eighteenth century mansion as a middle-aged man sits at a Steinway grand in a magnificently decorated baroque room. His passion has been to play piano since a small boy, and now in his sixties, he plays with consummate dexterity. At the end of his favourite Nocturne in E^{b}, there is a knock at the drawing room door. A butler opens the double doors and enters to deliver a message to his employer.

"Shall I bring Mr Bentley in now, Sir?" the butler asks the man at the piano.

"Ah, splendid. Have him join me for dinner, Rodrigues."

"Yes sir", replies the butler. He bows and leaves the room.

Bentley is assisted to the bathroom to freshen up before dinner with his host. At eight o'clock the butler escorts him to the dining room, where he meets the pianist and owner of the mansion. As he is led into the room he sees the long dining table in the centre of the sumptuously decorated room. The walls are faced with oak panelling and above classical murals adorn the ceiling.

"Mr Bentley – how good of you to join me for dinner. Please take a seat", invites the man at the other end.

"This way sir", says Rodrigues and pulls back a chair at the opposite end of the table.

"Where am I, and who are you?" enquires Bentley.

"My name is Kapultski, and you are my guest in my villa in Madeira".

"Madeira?" asks Bentley.

"All will be explained in due course. But first – please select your choice from our exquisite menu. Rodrigues – an aperitif for our guest".

Bentley studies the menu. He hasn't eaten for many hours and can't imagine being poisoned by his host now. When Rodrigues comes over, Bentley gives him the starter and main course order.

"Carpaccio, followed by halibut steak, with sweet potato and artichoke hearts, please"

"An excellent choice Mr Bentley – and may I suggest a 1985 Chablis to go with it?" Kapultski asks.

"Thank you - that will be fine" answers Bentley.

The butler takes Kapultski's order, and exits the room.

"Now Mr Bentley – you must be wondering how you came to be in Madeira".

"Yes, the thought had crossed my mind", replies Bentley.

"I'd like you to tell me who you are and what you know about my operation".

"Oh come now – haemorrhoids isn't such a big deal these days".

That answer only served to elicit a leaden glower from Kapultski.

"Lafarge asked you to perform a certain task in Marrakesh, but you failed spectacularly".

"On the contrary, my mission was an unrivalled success", replies Bentley. "Where is Lafarge – are you an associate of his?"

"Lafarge was one of my managers, but he has been released from the service on the grounds of ill health".

"What was wrong with his health?" asks Bentley.

"He had the unfortunate affliction of a bullet in the brain".

Rodrigues enters with the starters. Bentley sips his Noilly Prat as Rodrigues brings the first course of mussels to Kapultski, and then the carpaccio to Bentley. Rodrigues pours the Chablis, first to Kapultski, then leaves the room.

"You were told that if you did not kill Marengo, you would die. Instead of killing him you gave him the greatest warning possible that he was subject to an assassination attempt, and if it had not been that our men were at the bottom of the tower, you would have escaped".

"I'm afraid you are wrong in two ways. Firstly as an agent for British Intelligence it was my mission to prevent the murder of President Marengo. Our Government believes that he can bring stability to the DRC and stop the country from sliding into civil war again. Secondly, I couldn't wait for the police to find me in the clock tower, so I made my escape in order to reach the café as planned. I wouldn't have tried to escape because the second part of my mission was to learn more about your operation, and here I am, discussing it with you, face to face".

"You mean to tell me you would risk your life in order to deliberately bring about a meeting with me?" Kapultski starts to laugh. "You must have an enormous amount of faith and courage".

"I'm here as an agent for Her Majesty Queen Elizabeth of the United Kingdom. That's all the faith and courage I need", Bentley replies confidently.

After some time Rodrigues enters with the main courses on a trolley. He removes the starter plates and places the entrees accordingly. After pouring more wine for both, he exits.

"You must be a very patriotic man Mr Bentley – or should that be idiotic? You have unswerving faith in a country that has nothing to offer the world. What contribution has Britain made to the world in the past hundred years? Britain is nothing but a poodle that the United States likes to stroke now and then."

"How about winning the second world war? Without the British Hitler would have conquered the world with the help of the Japanese," Bentley asserts.

"The British were just lucky the Japanese bombed Pearl Harbour and forced the Americans to join the war."

"And did you ever wonder why the Japanese bombed Pearl Harbour?" asks Bentley. "They couldn't possibly defeat the Americans by bombing one naval base. Why would they have deliberately provoked America to join the war?"

"I'm interested to hear your theory, Mr Bentley."

"It's no theory Kapultski. British Intelligence managed to get a coded message to Tokyo on the 6th of December 1941 to say Japan would be attacked the following day. So good was British Intelligence that the Japanese took the message seriously and launched a pre-emptive strike on Pearl Harbour, and successfully brought America into the war, and as you so rightly say, without America we would have lost the war."

"But this is pure fantasy – no historian, no politician and no conspiracy theorist has ever suggested that the British were behind the bombing of Pearl Harbour".

"Well we certainly wouldn't want this information to be leaked to the United States."

Kapultski is surprised by Bentley's statement. After a period of silence, he begins to question him again.

"So Mr Bentley – what is it you hope to achieve by meeting me?" he asks.

"We know about your plans to overthrow the elected president so you can set up a Quisling dictator who'll help you plunder the country of its resources of diamonds".

"Diamonds? Is that why you think I've gone to all the trouble of having an African president assassinated and a new dictator sworn in? For the sake of a few diamonds? Oh no, Mr Bentley. I've have other plans in mind instead of mining diamonds".

"It is because of your other plans that I have been sent here on an assignment for MI6. I want to ask you what is involved in these plans, because it affects international security".

"And what possible interest could anything you have to offer be to me?"

"My country is prepared to assist you with an unlimited financial backing to offset any action of yours which might jeopardise the global economy".

"Your offer of financial backing is of no interest to me. I have an enterprise of my own which requires no assistance from the British Government."

He has one more sip of wine and dabs his mouth with the serviette.

"Rodrigues – I'll skip dessert, but please give our guest anything he desires, and then make him comfortable in the Cavendish suite where he can spend the night. Please enjoy the rest of your dinner Mr Bentley - it was a very interesting conversation".

Leaving Rodrigues to replenish Bentley's glass, Kapultski bids him goodnight and leaves the dinner table.

Chapter 19

After dinner, two men escort Bentley to the Cavendish suite. Inside the room is bare, with only a single bed and a table. There is no window and one fluorescent light overhead. The two men leave him in the room as they turn and exit. The locking of the door has a loud, mechanical sound. The voices die away, and Bentley sits on the bed. What did Kapultski intend by overthrowing the President and replacing him with a puppet dictator? If it wasn't for diamonds as Lafarge thought, what could it have been?

It is rather cool inside his cell, but fortunately the men gave him back the jacket which he was wearing at the clock tower. It is a casual linen jacket, with a felt patch on the right shoulder. As he sits on the edge of the bed, he begins inspecting the shoulder patch, and fingers around the stitching at the edges. He comes across one loose end of a thread, just under the lapel. He begins to pull the thread which eventually unravels until the whole thread can be drawn out. The patch comes away from the jacket, leaving the shoulder material unaffected beneath. He looks at the patch and turns it over. The underside shows two small flat packets, in sealed plastic, and in different colours, so thin they could not be seen under the patch. Bentley peels away the small plastic sheets from the patch, and then feels around under the lapel. There, a small spare button is located, as if to hold the collar together when turned up in cold weather. The thread holding it on is weak, and it is removed from the underside of the lapel by a quick tug.

Laying his jacket on the table he goes over to the door. He tears away the red plastic from the first pack. Inside there is a soft whitish material similar in appearance to putty. He kneads it between his fingers and shapes it around the lock of the door. He holds the button in his left hand, gives it a quarter turn with his right, and pushes it into the soft material. He pulls the mattress over to the door and then places the table behind the mattress. With his jacket over his head he crouches in the opposite corner. Five seconds later a blast blows the door wide open with a loud bang and flash, and the cell is filled with smoke. He fumbles for the green packet and stands behind the open door.

The guard runs in, his rifle at waist level. Bentley's left hand seizes the muzzle of the rifle and forces it to point to the floor. With his right hand he holds a cotton pad to the guard's nose and mouth. The guard struggles and brings his left hand up to pull Bentley's hand away, but in a few seconds the man has been overcome with ether fumes and falls to the floor.

Bentley grabs his jacket, runs through the doorway, along a short corridor in the basement of the house, lifts the latch on the outer door and escapes into the cobbled courtyard. Others in the house must have heard the explosion, so he must quickly find the way to get out of the courtyard. He runs up to the main gate. Behind him he is in full view from the big house. Through the locked gates he can see the ocean way below. It is a moonlit night and he will be easily seen in this light. He looks around for a means of escape. He hears the crashing of the waves on the rocks below as he searches for any possible way out.

"Over here!" He hears a woman's voice speaking in a loud whisper. "Over here!" she calls. With his back against the perimeter wall he creeps towards a side gate from where the voice came. As he reaches the single gate a young woman stands on the other side of the bars. In the moonlight he sees she is a pretty girl in her late teens with dark hair, and she is holding something in her hand.

"Quickly! They'll be here soon!" she says as she starts to open the steel gate.

"Who *are* you?" he asks under his breath.

"Never mind that now", she replies. "This is your wallet and passport. Go to the top cable car station at ten tomorrow. A man will be waiting for you to take you to Gibraltar."

"How will I know him?"

"He'll know you", and with that she disappears into the shadows.

He puts the wallet and passport into his jacket and heads for the trees a hundred metres from the house.

Chapter 20

The ocean shimmers with an azure iridescence as the cable car climbs its way up the hill above Funchal old town. Bentley managed to find a quiet guest house for the night, and has freshened up after having bought a few things before breakfast.

Burnt orange roof tiles and a profusion of plants and flowers are revealed beneath the cable car, and people far below go about their daily business; setting up tables at an outdoor cafe, arranging fruit and vegetables at a market stall, or unwinding the mooring rope way down at the harbour before a day's fishing.

Eventually the cable car arrives at the station at the top of the hill. Bentley tentatively looks around as he steps out. This is the place where he is to meet the contact who will arrange for him to be taken to Gibraltar, and perhaps may explain what Kapultski is planning.

His fellow passengers chat and laugh as they step out of the cable car. It is a bright, fresh morning high above the town, and hilltops farther up disappear into a grey haze of low cloud. Minutes go by and the next cable car brings another group to the upper station. The voices die away again leaving only the sound of birdsong and light breeze. Bentley looks around. Now there is no one in sight. Who was the girl last night, and why had she helped him? If she were not to be trusted she could have raised the alarm at the house, and he would have been recaptured in an instant. If the meeting with the contact were to fall through, he would have no other avenue to explore. The trail would go cold and he would never know what Kapultski had in mind. Another cable car arrives and a group of tourists disembark. Will the man be here this time? Once again people wander off away from the cable car station, but there is no sign of the man sent to help him. All is quiet as Bentley continues to wait.

A car appears behind him, making its way up the steep hill. Eventually a third cable car releases its passengers, and again the air is filled with chatter and laughter. Then, through the passing group of tourists he notices two men and a woman studying the tourists as they walk past. It's the girl from last night. Are these two men, tall and dressed in dark suits, going to take him to Gibraltar?

"There he is!" the girl suddenly shouts as she spots Bentley. The men look across and immediately begin running towards him.

"That's the man – get him!" the girl cries.

Bentley takes off down the hill, past the Japanese garden with the two men in pursuit. The girl now bursts out laughing and runs after the men to keep up with the action. Now at full speed downhill, the men begin closing on Bentley. This isn't the assistance he was expecting, he thinks as he races down the narrow cobbled street. All he can hear is the loud clatter of feet, his own panting and the girl's peals of laughter. People casually carrying groceries up the hill or old ladies sweeping their doorsteps turn in dumbstruck astonishment as the three men career past them, with the girl following behind.

He must find a way out of this fast, but there is nowhere to go to shake of his pursuers. He turns another corner. There ahead of him some people are standing in the middle of the road beside what looks like some large flat baskets. As he grows closer it becomes clear what the people are doing. He has arrived at the point where tourists are being pushed down the winding cobbled streets of Funchal in toboggans; little wicker cars for two with runners, like dry sledges with two gondoliers dressed in traditional Portuguese costumes who push and steer the passengers down the steep and twisting street to the foot of the hill.

The tourists and toboggan pilots now hear and catch sight of the bizarre scene of three men racing downhill at breakneck speed with a girl trying to keep up and laughing hysterically all the way. They stand agape as Bentley approaches. In the toboggan all ready for departure, a slightly- built elderly English lady sits, with a pilot left and right behind her. She strains to look behind to see what is causing all the commotion. The gondoliers are frozen in time. Bentley fumbles with his jacket and pulls out his wallet. He jumps over the back of the toboggan between the two men and lands on the seat next to the startled lady.

"Here's a hundred each – get us out of here fast!" as he flashes two hundred euro bills at them.

"Pardon me madam – nothing worse than travelling alone", he comments to his newly-acquired toboggan partner.

No sooner have the men stuffed the notes into the pockets of their white trousers, and with the pursuers now only a few metres away, the toboggan takes off on its rapid, downward descent. People are aghast as the impromptu drama unfolds. Now instead of thundering feet, the sound is of the runners gliding along the cobbles and the men's feet steering the toboggan around the corners.

Behind, the two pursuers have reached the toboggans and have commandeered the next in line for departure. Fortunately they do not have the company of a gracious granny, and rather than by financial persuasion, their method is to pull guns on the toboggan pilots, now press-ganged into service. As they speed away, the girl stands watching the action, convulsed with laughter.

The two toboggans are now flying downhill as if it were an Olympic sport, with the men straining to control the course of the wicker carriages. As they approach the bends the toboggans spin round sideways, like fairground waltzers. The wooden runners over the cobbles and men's boots used for braking as corners approach, cause a loud, rumbling, rattling noise, like skateboards a hundred years ahead of their time. Onlookers' frozen faces flash by as the toboggans twist and turn on their tortuous descent.

"My word!" utters Mrs Blancheflower, as the toboggans slalom round oblique bends at a fearsome speed. The haste of the leading toboggan is sharpened considerably by the sight of the guns which are being pointed at the two pilots behind.

"Faster! Faster!" one of the gunmen yells at the pilots and threatens them with his weapon. The benhuresque chariot scene takes a turn for the worse when gunshots start to ring out and ricochet off walls and houses.

"Goodness me!" comments Mrs Blancheflower as the pilots try to duck the volley of bullets.

A right-angled bend approaches. They'll have to slow down for the corner and that's when the gunmen will kill them. Closer...closer...the toboggans roar downhill as they approach the house at the bend. They can't escape now. More shots are fired from behind, and again the gondoliers duck involuntarily. The corner arrives and the first toboggan slides sideways past the old house. Now the pursuers – just at the point of turning the pilots leap for their lives from each side of the speeding toboggan. With no pilots to steer it the toboggan runs out of control and hits the kerb, and as the back of the toboggan flies upwards, the gunmen are catapulted head-first and crash through the toilet window on the first floor.

Bentley's toboggan comes to rest safely at the bottom of the hill. He steps out, thanks the men, and helps his lady friend out of the carriage.

"That must have been paneful", he comments to an ashen-faced Mrs Blancheflower.

Chapter 21

Bentley continues on his way down to the main road. He'd given his would-be captors the slip, but what now? Who was that crazy girl who had helped him escape from Kapultski's villa, only to betray him at the cable car station? Now he'd have to find a way of getting away from Madeira without Kapultski's henchmen stopping him. Once again the trail had gone cold and he was at a loss to uncover the mystery that had courted him. A little farther on he arrives at the entrance to Reid's Palace, the exclusive nineteenth century hotel where such famous guests as Winston Churchill, George Bernard Shaw and Gregory Peck had visited.

He could relax for an hour while having lunch, and enjoying the magnificent view of the bay from the open terraced tearoom. The waiter brings him lapsang souchong and a glass of claret, before his lunch of duck a l'orange. Now there's no way of ever knowing what sinister plans Kapultski had in mind. At least he can sit quietly and just enjoy lunch amid the chatter of other guests who have come to Reid's.

An hour comes and goes, and he slowly finishes his tea, pays the waiter and strolls towards the front door of the hotel. He turns to the right, down the hill towards Funchal town centre. Maybe the best thing would be to get a taxi to the airport and get the next flight out of Madeira. Suddenly he becomes aware of a car approaching at speed behind him. With the screech of tyres a black four-door Porsche Panamera pulls up abruptly. One man gets out from the nearside back seat, another from the road side.

Without a word, Bentley jumps up onto the bonnet, stamps the offside passenger on the chest and races across the road. A single-decker bus lumbering up the hill provides a few seconds distance between him and the pursuing men. He just clears the front of the bus as the driver blows his horn in protest. Just across the pavement a narrow lane lies in front of him. It has brick walls on each side, and open at the top. He takes the opportunity and runs off along the lane with the men just managing to get across the busy road, accompanied by a short cacophony of horns. But then in front of him he could see no exit – just a brick wall. Is it a dead-end, he momentarily thinks? The men behind are running down the lane. He gets to the end of the lane – but it isn't a dead end. The lane has a right-angle bend to the left and continues for another hundred metres or so. He can see the exit of the lane ahead. Gasping now, he runs at full speed, with the men closing on him behind. He gets to the exit and out into the street. All clear he thinks – but no. The moment he hits the street a white Alfa Giulietta pulls up sharply right in front of him. Now he is cornered. The men behind haven't reached the bend yet. Only the driver sits in the Alfa on the other side away from the pavement, with the window down.

"Get in!" he shouts.

"Who are you?" Bentley asks hurriedly.

"Quick – they'll be here any moment. Get in!"

"How can I trust you?" he asks the man, and glances back along the lane.

"You can't!" is his reassuring reply.

He opens the front door and gets in. The Alfa accelerates away from the lane just as the men are turning the corner. Bentley breathes a loud sigh of relief but then asks himself what more trouble has he got into now.

The driver is a young man in his twenties, dark hair, small and slim. If he is part of the gang, why is he alone? Is he going to trick him and take him back to the villa?

"Who are you?" he asks the man again.

"My name is Angelo – Angelo Kapultski", he replies.

Bentley feels a cold flush come over him.

"I believe you had dinner with my father?" the man continues.

"Your father is Kapultski?"

"That's right – and my sister is Odile. You had the pleasure of meeting her outside the villa after your escape and then at the cable car station".

"I see - and where are we going now? Back to the villa?"

This is a situation that Bentley can't countenance – not with just one man in the car. His next action will be to seize the wheel and force the car to crash into a wall or tree, and he'll make his escape then. He clasps his seatbelt. He glances down between the seats. The man is not wearing his seat belt.

Several times the driver glances up at the rear-view mirror as if to check if he is being followed.

"We're not going to the villa", the man replies. "We're going to the harbour."

"Why the harbour?" Bentley enquires.

"There's a boat waiting to take you to Gran Canaria, and get you off the island."

"If you're Kapultski's son, why would you want to get me off the island?"

"Father and son don't always get on – do they?"

"And your sister – why did she help me escape only to trick me in the morning?"

"Because it amused her to play a silly game with you. She's just an immature fool, but Daddy gives her everything she wants."

"But you don't get the same treatment?" Bentley asks as the car continues on its way to the harbour, so far unnoticed by Kapultski's men.

"No he doesn't – in fact he doesn't even like me. It was always Odile he favoured, never me. He was never proud of me no matter what I did. Odile has the brain of a ten year old, but she's always been Daddy's little girl. He never had a kind word for me."

"You're not going to play the same trick on me that your sister did are you?"

"I don't know what kind of dubious business my father is involved in, but I've seen some very shady things go on over the years, and I'm taking a big chance by letting you escape", Angelo explains.

"What kind of business is he supposed to be in?" asks Bentley.

"I've said enough already. You don't need to know any more. Just get on the boat that's waiting for you, and when you get to Las Palmas you get a plane back to Britain and forget you ever came here."

The car pulls into the harbour entrance and stops alongside a green, medium-sized rusty cargo boat used for carrying sacks of wheat or flour in its hold. Along the prow the words 'Pride of Valletta' are painted in white. Bentley can just make out the back of the pilot standing at the wheel, looking out to sea. There doesn't seem to be anyone else on deck.

“Get on board”, Angelo advises Bentley. “My father’s men might be looking for you down here, and I wouldn’t just get my pocket money suspended if they knew I’d helped you.”

“I’m indebted to you for helping me”, Bentley says as he steps out of the car and scans the road along the harbour. “Maybe we’ll meet again one day”.

“Maybe we will”, Angelo replies as he turns away and accelerates back to the main road.

Bentley watches the white Alfa drive away, and then he turns and walks up the small gangway onto the boat. An old man with a white beard pulls the gangway off the boat, lifts the rope from the capstan and throws it onto the deck. With a short call to the pilot, the engine revs up and the boat heads out to sea.

Bentley stands looking back to Funchal as it gets farther and farther away, bewildered by the day’s events. Now at least he is safe. He has nothing more to go on, and all that remains was to catch a plane home when he gets to Las Palmas.

Chapter 22

As the town drifts away into the distance Bentley feels relieved to be on board the boat that is taking him to safety. The engine drones hypnotically and the wash rushes behind the boat, and some time passes as he collects his thoughts and eventually turns away from the island. He can make out the pilot through the rear window of the wheelhouse, his hands on the wheel, and wearing a blue boiler suit and cap. He is looking ahead out to sea as Bentley opens the door and goes across to introduce himself.

"Hi", he says as he enters. The pilot turns round. A sudden expression of surprise is revealed on Bentley's face. It isn't a male pilot at all. It's a girl who is at the wheel. She smiles at Bentley as she says "Welcome aboard."

Her dark hair and brown eyes give her a Mediterranean appearance. She is quite tall, and with looks that Bentley immediately finds attractive. She bends over to open a small cupboard door in front of the wheel and brings out a bottle and two glasses.

"Here – pour us a couple of glasses of blueberry grappa. You'll find some ice in the fridge behind you. Bentley takes the bottle and glasses and looks behind him for the fridge. He begins pouring out the grappa into the glasses.

He hands one glass to the pilot.

"Buona salute!" she says as she raises her glass.

"Good health!" is his English reply to her.

"The name's John Bentley. Thanks for letting me come with you."

"I'm Fiorenza. Glad to help you", and she turns again to look out to sea.

"May I sit here with you?" he asks politely.

"Of course – make yourself at home. It'll be a long time before we reach Las Palmas."

The cargo vessel slowly makes its way out to open sea and Bentley casually looks ahead at the unbroken horizon as he sips his grappa. The danger of Madeira was behind him now, thanks to

Angelo who had secured a crossing for him to Gran Canaria. The pilot continues to steer the boat as she looks out to sea.

"How do you know Angelo?" he eventually asks the girl.

"He was my boyfriend a few years ago", she replies still looking ahead.

"He did me a big favour fixing up this boat trip".

"Yes he has a good heart."

"Why would he do that for me?" Bentley asks.

The girl looks round at him. "He and his sister don't get on, and he doesn't approve of some of the things his father has done in the past."

"What sort of business is his father in?"

"They say he's the director of an online banking organisation in Geneva. Madeira's just his holiday home."

"Why would the director of a Swiss bank want an African president assassinated?" he asks rhetorically.

"I can't say more than that. I just do this run from Funchal to Las Palmas delivering various products, sacks of cereal, rice, sometimes coffee, sometimes barrels of beer."

They settle back into silence again as the boat engine rumbles away beneath them. Time dwindles away and eventually the Islas Desertas slowly pass by on the port side as the boat heads south towards Gran Canaria. The hours drift by as they talk casually about her family, her home in Palermo, how she came to be the pilot on a boat off the Moroccan coast.

"If you want to rest, there's a bunk below deck on the right", the pilot says after some time.

"Yes, I'd like to do that", he answers.

After a while Bentley goes to the stern and looks out over the wash. He reflects on the situation he had wandered into. When he gets to Las Palmas it will be the end of the line. He might as well relax now he thinks, as he wanders up to the bow. The pilot holds a steady course as the ship continues steaming to the port of Santa Catalina in Las Palmas.

Below deck he finds the bunk the pilot suggested he used. It's a very welcome rest and he is soon lulled to sleep by the monotonous drone of the engine. Now at last he can relax in safety.

After about an hour he awakes to the sound of the engine being turned over. It becomes quiet, and then the sound of the engine turning over again. It must have cut out. The girl tries again, but it still won't fire. All he can hear is the lapping of the waves around the boat and then the engine turning over. He gets up from the bunk and goes into the wheelhouse to ask what had happened.

"What's the trouble?" he asks her.

"I don't know – it just cut out and now it won't start again."

"Do you want me to have a look at the engine?"

"Yes, we better see what's wrong. Down the stairs under the deck".

Bentley goes down the stairs beneath the wheelhouse and opens the heavy steel door. Inside it's dark and oily. There's a switch by the door which lights up a single swinging bare light bulb. It's a dirty room with some spanners lying on a work bench against the wall. He has to throw some wooden crates out of the way before he can see the engine. It's a six cylinder petrol engine with spark plugs. He recognises it as an old fifties truck engine which has Chevrolet embossed on the rocker cover, adapted to drive a propeller for marine use. It reminds him of the same old straight six that he had in his hot rod when he was in his twenties.

The first idea he has is that it might have run out of petrol. He shouts up to her "What does the fuel gauge read?"

"Half full" she shouts back.

Might be a faulty gauge he thinks, and goes to the tank on the opposite wall from the tools. He opens the filler cap and with the help of a hand-held lamp, he can see fuel inside. Maybe a faulty fuel pump, is his next idea. With one of the spanners he disconnects the fuel line.

"Turn her over" he shouts up.

A spurt of petrol indicates that there is nothing wrong with the pump.

"I've made some coffee", shouts Fiorenza from the wheelhouse.

Away in the distance, a ship becomes visible, no more than a dot on the horizon. Bentley sits chatting to the girl as they sip their coffees.

"Unusual taste the coffee has", he comments.

"Yes I put rum in it".

"Nice flavour. Are you always alone on the boat?" he asks.

"Oh no, Pedro is usually here. He works in the engine room and helps unload the cargo", she answers.

"Where is he today?"

"He couldn't come in because he drank too much at the weekend".

"But it's Thursday today."

"Goodness – Thursday already!"

"Does he look after the engine?" Bentley enquires.

"Yes, he looks after all the mechanical things. Last week he told me he was having trouble fitting the coil on top of the dynamo – something about a little cylinder on top of a big one".

He continues sipping the coffee and thinking about the engine. The ship that was just a dot on the horizon is nearer now. They can see it's a large container vessel.

"That's a big ship up ahead – must be a hundred thousand tons. What do you think's in those containers?" he asks casually.

"Luxury cars – Jaguars, Mercedes, BMWs. The cars I'll never have".

"Maybe it's a cargo of diamonds, gold and silver".

"Like the jewellery I'll never have".

"Try the engine again", Bentley suggests.

Fiorenza goes over to the wheel and presses the starter button. The engine turns over, more slowly than before. The engine still won't start. He goes back down to the engine room again. In the corner lies an outboard motor, too small to run the boat properly; presumably just for emergencies. If all else fails, he can connect up the outboard motor and head for the nearest port.

If it isn't a fuel problem it has to be electrical, he surmises as he pulls off one of the spark plug leads. He finds a pair of insulated pliers and holds the open end of the lead half an inch from the rocker cover. If there's a spark, he'll see it flash.

"Give her another go", he shouts upstairs.

The engine turns over again, this time even slower. There is no spark. He notices, as Fiorenza had said, that the coil is held underneath the dynamo at the front of the engine, tied together with a piece of string. He feels the terminals of the coil. They seem secure -

maybe the coil's faulty. He finds another coil in Pedro's oily crate of spare parts, but after connecting it up still no spark is seen. Bentley tries everything he can think of to fire up the engine.

"Better fix it quick", shouts Fiorenza. "Look how close the ship is now", warns the girl.

The ship is only a mile away, and they seem to have wandered into a main shipping channel. The container ship is on collision course, and their boat is drifting right towards it.

"Better get on the radio and send a distress message", Bentley advises.

"Okay I'll call the international emergency frequency", she answers.

"I'll go back down and try again", he tells her as she calls the emergency channel.

"Mayday, Mayday", she calls over the radio.

"Emergency rescue channel – come in please", she hears through the radio.

"We're about 200 miles off the Moroccan coast. The engine's failed and we've drifted into the path of a container ship. Can you try to alert the ship?" she asks the service operator.

"What's your position?" the man on the radio asks.

"16 degrees longtitude by 29 minutes", she replies.

"Calling the ship's emergency channel now", the man tells her.

Back down in the engine room Bentley tries frantically to understand why there is no spark. He double-checks again but still can't find the problem.

"Try her again!" he shouts upstairs.

The engine turns over lazily, but still won't start. He runs back up to the wheelhouse. The ship is only half a mile away.

"I've tried everything – I can't think of what else to do", explains Bentley, now gravely concerned at the looming sight of the container ship.

"The container ship is not responding to our signal", the voice on the radio announces. "I'll keep trying"

"Hurry!" she shouts to the emergency channel. "The ship's going to hit us!"

"Surely they can see us – give them a few blasts on the horn", Bentley tells her. Fiorenza presses the klaxon but all that is heard are a few barely audible peeps.

"What's happened to the horn?" he asks.

"The main horn broke down but Pedro found a horn from a Cinquecento in a scrap yard in Livorno", she explains.

"What about flares?"

"Never had any".

"How about the outboard motor – does it work?"

"Pedro meant to fix it but he never got round to it"

The ship advances with the distant drone of the massive engines as she heads inexorably straight towards them. The ship is only two hundred metres away.

"We better get ready to abandon ship – where are the life jackets?" he asks.

"Behind you in the locker."

"We're going to abandon ship!" she shouts down the radio. "Send a helicopter to pick us up!" She throws down the handset as Bentley hands her a life jacket. All around is the vast storm grey expanse of the ocean, with no other ship in sight.

"Put this on – any longer and we'll be sucked under the propellers". He puts his own life jacket over his head and then helps her tie her straps.

"Let's get ready to jump", he tells her.

"Is the engine no good?" she asks in desperation.

"I can't get a spark. I don't know why - the only thing that's out of place is the coil, but the connections are okay"

"That's what Pedro fixed last week – the little cylinder on top of the big one next to the fan".

"Let's get ready!" he tells her.

Through the window the bow of the ship is towering over the boat. It is going to hit them in a few minutes. They must jump now if they have any chance of swimming out of the way of the leviathan's propellers. The throbbing of the ship's engine is getting louder and louder.

"Let's go before they hit us," he shouts.

The deck of the cargo boat had become dark with the threatening sight of the ship bearing down on them. Where were the crew? Why had they not seen their boat? Was no one on the bridge?

They run to the stern of the boat. The collision would be any minute. Fiorenza looks afraid at what is about to happen. Bentley takes her hand.

"Good luck Fiorenza! I hope we survive!"

"Stay close to me when we jump!" she replies.

Suddenly the horns of the container ship start booming out long, deep, deafening blasts. He takes her hand and they steel themselves for the ordeal that is about to occur. They are ready to jump when suddenly a thought flashes through his mind.

"What did you just say?" he hurriedly asks her. "The little cylinder on top of the big one?"

"Quickly – let's jump!" she shouts.

The foghorns bellow again, now even louder.

"But it was the other way round", he remembers.

"Come on!" she cries.

He turns and looks back towards the bow. The huge red hull of the container ship is almost on top of them. It is too late to jump. He races back to the wheelhouse and runs down the stairs into the engine room. He looks at the coil underneath the dynamo. He feels under the coil. It is loose and has slipped down under the dynamo instead of on top. He runs his fingers along the earth lead from the coil to the distributor. Halfway along he feels the damage to the cable. It has burned through after touching the hot exhaust pipes, and the bare wires are showing at each end. He can hear the thundering sound of the ship's engines above. He runs upstairs and shouts to the girl.

"Quickly! Go to the wheelhouse!" he shouts back to the girl.

She runs back to the wheelhouse. He holds the two ends of the cable together with the bare wires touching.

"Try her now!" he shouts. She presses the starter as the gargantuan size of the ship fills the window. The engine turns over very slowly. No sign of life. The deep roar from the foghorns causes the wheelhouse to shudder.

"Again!"

She presses the button as he holds the bare wires between his fingers downstairs. The turn-over gets slower. They're going to be hit any moment. She keeps her finger on the button.

"Come on! Come on!" Bentley shouts.

The engine coughs and tries to fire. She keeps pressing the button. The engine tries to fire. Then it does. The engine bursts into life.

"Get us out of here!" he shouts.

She pulls the wheel hard over to starboard at full speed. The vessel slowly lumbers to the right and passes the bow of the container ship with inches to spare. The Pride of Valletta slips past the enormous hull of the ship and as the girl steers on full lock, the waves from the wash buffet the boat so violently that it is almost overturned by the strength of the displacement. They are tossed around relentlessly as the boat lurches from one side to the other. Bentley is thrown across the engine room, but has managed to tape the two wires together. The container ship sails on and glides past them. Fiorenza manages to get control of the boat at last and eventually the waves die down. The container ship continues on her way across the North Atlantic and the throbbing of the engines drifts into the distance.

Bentley takes a very deep breath as the girl steers the boat into calmer waters. For a few minutes they are silent as they reflect on the narrow escape. They both sigh deeply with the shock of the experience.

"Better get out the rum", suggests Bentley as they sail calmly again.

He pours out a couple of large glasses and eventually she speaks.

"That was close!" Fiorenza remarks.

They clink glasses and sip the rum and coke.

"Well done Fiorenza! What a skipper!"

"Well done Mr Bentley!" she says with a smile. "What a mechanic!"

Chapter 23

The cargo boat continues to steam towards the port of Santa Catalina in Las Palmas. Several hours go by since the mysterious encounter with the container ship. Bentley's experience of souping up cars and hot rods as a young man had finally saved his life, and that of Fiorenza, with whom he suddenly has a dramatic change of relationship.

The sun is beginning to set as they eventually see Las Palmas in the distance. It has been a long and eventful voyage from Madeira. The boat begins to slow down. When it comes to a halt half a mile from Santa Catalina bay, Fiorenza drops anchor.

"Why are we stopping here?" he asks.

"Well Mr Bentley," she replies. "Before we get to the harbour and have to say goodbye, I thought you might care to join me for a glass of port in my cabin."

"Yes of course – I'd be delighted."

She cuts the engine, and all is quiet again apart from the lapping of the waves around the boat.

"I'll just go and freshen up. Meet me below deck in ten minutes," she suggests.

"See you then", he replies.

Dusk is falling over Las Palmas. Bentley looks out towards Santa Catalina harbour in the distance. Several large ships are berthed outside the city. Bentley and Fiorenza have been very lucky not to have been sent to the seabed by the enormous red monster of the ocean. Thankfully that adventure is all over, and he is about to have a farewell drink with the skipper and then be on his way. After a while he makes his way below deck to her cabin. He gives a couple of knocks on the door, to which she replies "It's open".

The sight that greets him however is not what he had imagined. Fiorenza is no longer wearing the blue boiler suit, but instead her long black hair has been loosened and falls around her shoulders. She is wearing a large white shirt as she sits on the extended bunk which has been opened up into a double bed. She rests her back against a pillow, and the shirt is open by two or three buttons to reveal the cleavage of her large breasts. Her legs are crossed at the ankle.

"Well you seem to have changed into something more comfortable", he comments on entering the softly-lit cabin.

"Please pour us some port", she asks him and points to the bottle on a table by the bunk. He fills the two glasses and sits beside her on the edge of the open bunk.

"Well Fiorenza, it really has been quite an experience meeting you. Here's to the adventure we've had together". They clink their glasses and sip their drinks.

"The adventure, Mr Bentley, is only just beginning", she replies. "Why don't you get out of those clothes and come and sit up here with me". She kneels forward and begins undoing the buttons of his shirt. He passes his hand lightly under her shirt and over her breasts. With his other hand on her back they move forward and slowly their lips meet in a sensuous kiss.

"Come on in here with me," she whispers.

He removes his clothes and slips in beside her. Again they kiss, now more profoundly. He undoes the buttons of her long white shirt and slowly removes it. Their passion becomes stronger as they kiss and caress each other. He fondles her breasts and gently kisses her nipples, and then slowly moves down her body until his tongue overwhelms her with excitement.

"Come up to me now", she whispers after a while, and Bentley moves up until his knees are on either side of the pillow. "Now it's my turn", she says softly.

Their passion intensifies and now Bentley is on his back with Fiorenza astride him, her hands on his chest. She begins moving up and down, slowly to start with, and both are consumed with an unbelievably erotic sensation. Now faster and more energetically, they move into several different positions, increasing their ecstasy more and more, until eventually they arrive together in an explosion of unbridled passion.

Time passes luxuriantly as the cargo ship sways gently offshore from Santa Catalina. Seabirds soar in the sky, and dive into the sea. Occasionally a distant ship's horn sounds. On board, Bentley and Fiorenza lie peacefully after enjoying the blaze of sensuality as twilight falls.

"Well Mr Bentley", she says breathlessly. "You really are the best lover in the Atlantic".

"Call me John", he replies with a smile, and takes another sip of port. "And you're the prettiest skipper who ever sailed the Atlantic."

"Would you like to join me for dinner?" she asks Bentley.

"The last time I accepted such an invitation seismic tremors were recorded all around the world."

"This time it's just seafood chowder – want some?" she asks.

"I can't think of a more appealing idea", is his reply.

In the quietude of the evening, Fiorenza cooks dinner in the galley. Nightfall paints a nocturne of blue and gold around the harbour, and the lights of Las Palmas sway in the reflection of the water.

"It's quite a sight," he comments as he looks out towards the island.

"Yes it's pretty to see all the lights of Santa Catalina", Fiorenza replies as they sit down to dinner.

"Tomorrow I'll be going home to Britain without having been able to solve any of the mysteries that I've encountered since I left", he explains to her.

"I wish I could help you, but there's nothing more I know about it".

They sit at the table of the crew's quarters and enjoy Fiorenza's seafood chowder, accompanied by a bottle of Frascati.

"Do you know anything of Kapultski – his shady business dealings, what his ambitions are? I know he's planning something big; I just don't know what it is".

"There's only one person I know of who might be able to help you. His name is Tupelo Joe but he lives in Hong Kong".

"Who is he?" Bentley asks.

"He used to be Kapultski's chauffeur. I heard from Angelo that he left because he found out about the things Kapultski did to people. Kapultski used some really evil guy known as Abu the Beast to force people to pay money to him."

"How could I find Tupelo Joe?" Bentley asks.

"All I know is that he worked on the Star Ferry."

"Hong Kong's too far, and the information too weak. I could find nothing when I got there."

"I know", she replies.

"I'll be sorry to leave you tomorrow. It's been great to have spent a few days with you", he tells her.

"I'm going to miss you John", she answers. "I don't know you at all, but I feel I've always known you. I know you're a really good guy".

"One day you'll meet someone who'll treat you right and take you to nice places, out for nice meals, buy you nice things".

"Maybe one day", she replies pensively.

They relax with their meal and wine, and chat casually about a life at sea, and what hopes and dreams she has for the future. After dinner they retire to Fiorenza's cabin. Through the porthole they can see the lights of Las Palmas flicker in the waves, and some cargo ships wait outside the harbour to deliver their goods in the morning. Fiorenza will take Bentley into Santa Catalina harbour when they awake; she'll head back to Madeira and for Bentley it's the flight home to Britain with nothing achieved.

Chapter 24

It is a fragrant spring morning as Bentley casually strolls away from the North Pacific hotel and along Hennessy Road. The streets of Hong Kong are bustling with people, and the sounds of the city are an overture of clanking old British trams, the chatter of people going about their daily business, motorbikes and old red and white Toyota taxis.

He continues on his way, and as he crosses Luard Road two pretty Filipino girls catch hold of each arm to encourage him to pay a visit to their massage parlour. He politely smiles and says maybe another time. A tram takes him along to the Central District where he wanders up Stone Slabs Street, and enjoys the experience of the colourful outdoor fish and fruit markets along this historic street of flat granite flagstones. There's an exotic aroma of oriental spices in the air as he wanders along the busy street market stalls.

As the morning passes he eventually finds himself down by the harbour. On the other side of the bay are the skyscrapers of Kowloon, and at last Bentley can see the classic green and white boats of the Star Ferry crossing between the two terminals.

He buys a ticket and walks onto the landing platform. Who can he ask about Tupelo Joe, and what would he say if he does find him? He approaches one worker who is securing the mooring rope to one of the boats.

"Excuse me, does Tupelo Joe work here?" he asks the man.

"No name here", is the worker's curt reply. He looks around. Maybe someone on the ferry can tell him. He gets on board and waits for the journey across to Kowloon to begin.

The ferry finally starts up her engine and heads out across the bay. Looking back to Hong Kong Island he sees the iconic tower of the Bank of China with its distinctive diamond motifs, and the other buildings of the Finance District. The ferry reaches Kowloon terminal and before alighting he manages to say a few words to the pilot of the ferry.

"I'm looking for Tupelo Joe", he asks the pilot. The gruff response is much the same as before.

“Not know him”, is the sum total of his answer. What now?

An hour goes by and Bentley tries again and again to find out if anyone knows of Tupelo Joe. Each time he draws a blank. Maybe he never worked here. Maybe he left years ago. Maybe Fiorenza made a mistake. Back on the Hong Kong side he tries once more and again gets nothing but ‘no one here’ from one of the men throwing a rope onto a boat as it sails out of the harbour.

What can he do now? It seems no one has ever heard of him. Maybe he’d misheard the name from Fiorenza. Now there was nothing more he can do but admit defeat. Maybe tomorrow somebody might have heard of Tupelo Joe, but so far it’s been a disappointing day.

Back in the hotel he sleeps for an hour or two to shake off the jet lag, and it’s twilight before he eventually leaves the North Pacific for a walk through the city. If he can find those Filipinos again, maybe this time he’ll take them up on their invitation.

He’d heard of an old British pub on Lockhart Road with the very colonial name of The Trafalgar Bar. At least instead of Chinese lager he can get a decent pint of bitter. In this case it’s Old Speckled Hen. He sits up at the bar, slowly sips his pint of beer, and reflects on the failure of the day. Sometimes your luck just runs out, is all he can think now, as he finishes his first pint. He can try the Star Ferry tomorrow, but so negative was the response from everyone he spoke to, that he can’t imagine getting any farther forward. The barman pours another pint of Speckled Hen and Bentley pays and thanks him.

“Here on business or holiday?” the barman asks.

“Well it isn’t really either”, Bentley replies.

“Just been sightseeing?” the man asks politely.

“I came over here to try and find someone but I haven’t been able to”.

“Who is he?”

“Oh just some name I had. I thought he might give me some information that I needed. I was told he worked on the Star Ferry, but nobody has heard of him”.

“Have you come from Britain just to try and find him?”

"Well I got his name from a girl in Las Palmas, but she didn't know more than that."

"Must be pretty important to come all this way with only a name and where he might work", the barman says.

"It might be important, but I don't know for sure. I think some people's lives may be at risk and I was trying to prevent it, but I'm really just guessing."

"Why don't you just tell the police?" the barman asks.

"I haven't really got enough information. That's why I thought this man could help me", Bentley replies.

"What about the girl in Las Palmas?" the young barman asks casually, wiping the bar with a cloth.

"Her name is Fiorenza. She was the skipper of a cargo ship, and she said this man who worked on the Star Ferry could help me".

"It's a shame you've had a wasted journey".

"Well it's been great being in Hong Kong in the spring".

The barman goes to another side of the bar to serve a customer, and Bentley drinks his pint. I suppose Hong Kong will eventually lose all its Britishness now it's under Chinese rule he thinks, and finishes his second pint.

The barman returns and Bentley orders another one.

"Who was the guy anyway?" the barman asks.

"I only know his name was Tupelo Joe".

The barman continues drying a glass with a tea towel.

"Tupelo Joe is over there", is the barman's surprise revelation. He nods the direction of an alcove table at the side of the room where a man is sitting, facing the table with his head down. Bentley looks over but the man does not look up. Bentley lifts his drink and cautiously walks towards the table where the man is sitting.

"Tupelo Joe?" he asks the Chinese man at the table.

"Sit down please", the man offers. Bentley faces the man in the shadows at the alcove table. The man eventually looks up.

"What is it that you want?" he asks Bentley.

"A girl told me you could help me", he replies.

"Fiorenza – a lovely girl. It's been a long time since I've seen her. Does she still pilot the Pride of Valletta?"

"Yes she does. She helped me get away from Madeira. Some men were going to kill me and she let me sail with her to Las Palmas".

"Who was going to kill you?"

"His name is Kapultski. Fiorenza said you were his chauffeur but you didn't like the way he treated people."

"And what information are you looking for?"

"I believe that Kapultski's up to something very sinister. He tried to assassinate the president of a third world African country and I heard that many innocent people would die. I think he's going to try something like it again, but I don't know where or when it will be."

"I used to work for him", the man reveals. "But he's a very dangerous man, and I wanted to get as far away from him as possible. I've seen him inflict extreme violence on people. He employs someone who tortures people into parting with their homes and savings. They call him Abu the Beast. He's a sadistic psychopath. Keep away from him at all costs."

"But what is Kapultski's underworld business? What's he planning?" Bentley asks.

"I don't know, but if you can stop him I think you could save thousands of lives in Africa", says Tupelo Joe.

"What else can you tell me about what he might be doing?"

"He has some factory in Slovakia, in an industrial estate outside Bratislava. It's called Rubislav Engineering. Some kind of navigation equipment. Maybe you'll find something there."

"But what could that have to do with any operation in Africa?"

"That's all I can tell you. Don't come here again. I don't want Kapultski's men coming round here - I've got a wife and family. Now go".

"I don't know what I can do with that information, but thanks for speaking to me". Bentley stands up, and turns to walk away.

"There's just one thing", he asks the mysterious man in the shadows. "Where did you get the name Tupelo Joe from?"

"They used to say I could sing just like Elvis", he replies.

Bentley gives a faint smile and turns and walks out of the Trafalgar Bar and makes his way back to the hotel. It's night time in Hong Kong. As he walks through the Wan Chai district he wonders if the information he got from Tupelo Joe was any use at all. After a night at the North Pacific, he'll decide what he can do about the depot in Bratislava, and whether he should pursue the matter any further.

Chapter 25

It's mid-morning when Bentley arrives at the Rubislav industrial unit in Bratislava. For a while he walks around the place, trying to find what sort of operation is going on there. At the front there is a sign which reads 'Rubislav Printed Circuits' and nothing seems in any way unusual. Round the back there are two long, round chimneys made of concrete. They didn't seem to belong to the building – as if they'd been added on as an afterthought. Some heat haze seemed to come from the chimneys, but no smoke or steam.

Bentley continues to wander around casually as if waiting for a lift from someone. There are other units around the small industrial estate. Along the road a chuck wagon in the form of a stationary trailer is serving coffees and snacks to workers from nearby units.

Bentley has to get closer to see what's going on inside, but CCTV cameras cover the entire building. On one side there is a group of large oil drums and several pallets. If he could position them properly he could climb up and see through a window on the floor above. He could wait there all day, but sooner or later he'd have to bite the bullet and take a chance on the cameras.

Getting over the fence wasn't difficult, and after a minute he has arranged a few barrels, crates and pallets and is able to scale the impromptu climbing rig until he can see through the upstairs window. Better still, the window isn't locked, and he manages to open it and slip inside. On the other side of the window a steel gantry had been erected as an upper floor walkway, and here he can watch what is going on beneath without being noticed.

He crouches down close to the planks of the boardwalk and below he can see an incongruous sight which has little to do with the manufacture of printed circuits. On the ground floor some men are working, but they are wearing clothing that wouldn't have been out of place in a nuclear power station. They are completely covered from head to toe with astronaut-style helmets and separate breathing tanks on their backs. They appear to be pushing large wooden crates on roller gangways into two large furnaces. When a furnace door opens, another crate is pushed into the incandescent inferno and the heavy door is slammed shut again. The temperature is hot inside the plant and there is a strangely acrid smell.

Several wooden crates are stacked on top of one another, and other men are using forklift trucks to place the crates on the runners into the furnaces. What could be in these crates that requires such a high temperature to leave no smoke, and the men have to be dressed in such protective clothing? Why do they have to incinerate the wooden crates and their contents? He looks around the small unit for further information, but can see nothing else of importance. After fifteen minutes of observation he crawls back to the window and lowers his legs back onto the pile of pallets and oil drums. Suddenly he feels his ankles being gripped and he is dragged feet first down the makeshift platform and onto the tar surface below. As he looks up from the ground two men in black suits are standing above him.

"I think you'd better come with us", says one of the men in a broken English accent, and waves his gun towards a waiting car. They frisk him, then take him, one on either side to a black Audi A10, parked just outside the main gate. One man gets into the driver's seat on the left. The other opens the back door on the passenger side.

"Get in. We're going for a little drive", he tells Bentley.

Bentley is forced into the back of the car, and the man gets in after him.

"Where are you taking me?" he asks the men.

"We're going to meet a good friend", the man in the back says with a sleazy leer.

The car speeds away from the industrial estate and is soon on the open road.

"What were you doing inside the factory?" the man asks.

"Just a bit of casual sightseeing. The Tourist Office must've sent me the wrong way".

"Very amusing", the gunman replies. "However you might lose your sense of humour after our interrogation specialist has asked you a few questions. He has a way of teasing answers out of people."

"I'm not in the mood for a pub quiz at the moment", is Bentley's reply.

The driver laughs at Bentley's flippant remark.

"You do make us laugh. What a shame you won't be able to entertain us much longer. Unfortunately you have a date with Abu the Beast", says the man in the back.

Bentley feels an ice cold flush at the mention of Abu the Beast. This is the torturer that Fiorenza and Tupelo Joe told him to keep away from. The car travels along the country road. Few cars pass by on this remote route.

"What were the men burning in there?" asks Bentley.

"Some materials that the British would say were 'surplus to requirement'", the man replies.

"What kind of material?" Bentley continues.

"You ask a lot of questions", is the man's reply.

"Do you fear that I might escape?"

"Oh no – you won't escape."

"In that case you might as well tell me", Bentley asserts.

"We know who you are Mr Bentley. You've been causing the organisation a lot of trouble, and we're going to find out what you know and how much you've be telling the British Government".

"Why do you have to incinerate the crates at high temperatures like a crematorium?" Bentley goes on.

"Let's just say it's fertiliser that's gone past its sell-by date", and both men laugh at this remark.

Twenty minutes later the car pulls off the road and onto a dirt track where it stops. The man in the back says a few words in Slovak and walks away from the car and up the dirt track. He faces away from the car and starts to urinate into the barley.

Bentley starts to search for something in his jacket pocket. The driver becomes alarmed but Bentley assures him he is just looking for his cigarettes. He pulls out the pack and puts a cigarette in his mouth. The driver continues to stare at Bentley's every move. He cautiously offers the driver a cigarette. The driver accepts and takes out a cigarette and puts it in his mouth. Bentley is ready with the lighter and reaches across to light the driver's cigarette. The driver leans towards him, but instead of the lighter producing a flame, a loud hiss of gas is heard and the man immediately slumps unconscious onto the steering wheel, setting off the horn.

The other man has zipped up and runs back to the car. He catches sight of the driver and pulls out his pistol. The horn continues blaring. He runs over to the car and flings open the back door, pointing the gun at Bentley. With the cigarette still in his mouth he holds it between his fingers and blows the cigarette with one short puff. A poison dart hits the man in the neck. The man grasps his neck and drops his weapon. In seconds he is lying motionless on the ground.

Bentley quickly gets out of the car and pulls the driver off the steering wheel. The horn stops. He drags him onto the dirt track and across into the barley field. The other man is dragged into the field and dumped beside him. Bentley checks the men's pockets and finds their wallets. He leaves the money but removes other cards that might be useful. Ten seconds later he is at the wheel of the car, and he accelerates away from the scene leaving a cloud of dust behind him. He gets back onto the main road and half an hour later he has crossed the border and is in the safety of Austria.

Chapter 26

Somewhere to lie low for a few days. Somewhere where no one would think of looking. Somewhere like Munich.

Some research on the internet needed to be carried at the Hotel Am Markt where Bentley is staying, but before then a pleasant evening's relaxation is in order and he knows of a place not far from the hotel. The Augustiner on Neuhauser Strasse is a traditional Bavarian beer hall, steeped in history and tradition, where Bentley can sit quietly with a half-litre of dunkel beer, pork knuckle and sauerkraut, and in the company of several hundred German diners.

The huge hall plays no music, but the air is filled with chatter and laughter. No intimate cosy alcove table here – just join another dozen strangers round the large scrubbed oak table. The noisy atmosphere suits Bentley's mood, and he takes his time drinking beer and casually observing others in the thirteenth century beer hall.

Time passes and Bentley has another couple of dark beers. The dinner couldn't be considered sophisticated, but a straightforward, uncomplicated meal was what he had been looking forward to since flying in from Vienna. Eventually he makes his way through the old town, past Marienplatz and towards the market where the hotel is situated.

Back in his room he settles down with a glass of Cruzan rum which he'd managed to get at a tobacconist's on Talstrasse not far from the hotel. The television has many channels, but none is in English. In his wallet he takes out the ID cards from the two agents who had abducted him. They showed the names and photos of the operatives, and the company for whom they were employed. This was Lexoplein Pharmaceuticals, based in Helsinki. A quick search on his laptop brings up the company's website. He clicks on a few pages, but nothing out of the ordinary presents itself. The Home page gives an overview of the company as one would expect. The Business page gives details of the company's profits, turnover, directors' salaries, and other information. The Products page shows a list of the drugs manufactured by the company. This is leading nowhere. Nothing he had seen was in any way unusual.

He gets up and goes over to the window. He takes a sip of rum and watches people walking by in the cobbled street below. What would a couple of armed agents who had shoved him into the back of a car and who were taking him to be interrogated have to do with a pharmaceutical company? What were the men in protective clothing incinerating in the industrial unit in Bratislava, and how was it connected with this company called Lexoplein? He stands by the window as people go on their way, and sips his rum. The television continues to play in German.

Once again he studies the company website. He clicks on the heading of Vision. Objectives for the future...larger share of world market...effect on global economy... About two thirds down the page he finds a link. It's to a newspaper which carried a story on Lexoplein's quest to improve the standard of health in developing countries in Africa. He clicks on the link and a page appears from an African paper.

"Finnish pharmaceutical company Lexoplein to issue free drugs in a bid to eradicate disease among the poorest of Africa". What paper was this? A quick glance reveals the name – The Moroccan Times. So this company appeared to hold philanthropic beliefs and was in fact using its wealth to help the most destitute people in the third world. Altruistic though it may have been, it shed no light on why two armed thugs carried ID for the company. He looks away and tries to make some sense of it all. None of it gives the faintest clue about what had been going on at the industrial estate. Maybe there was nothing sinister after all. Maybe the men in space suits were just burning industrial waste. Maybe the armed men were just security guards who were going to release him after they'd removed him from the premises.

One more rum and then it's time for bed. Tomorrow he might stroll round the market, and stop somewhere for a coffee and Danish pastry. Then after that...

But what's this? A one-inch column at the foot of the page of the Moroccan Times catches his eye. It reads "Assassin to be Executed" and under the heading the text continues "A man who confessed that he attempted to assassinate President Marengo of the Democratic Republic of Congo is to be executed on Thursday. He had lain in wait with a high-powered rifle in the old clock tower in Toureag Square in Marrakesh when the DRC president arrived for an official state visit. Bonami Yassine will be taken from Oukacha Prison in Casablanca where he is being held, and taken to Rabat to be hanged."

Bentley looks up. They've rounded up someone to pin the attempted assassination of President Marengo on. The police must have picked up an innocent man and tortured him into confessing that he had tried to kill the president by shooting him from the clock tower. Today is Monday. They are going to execute him in less than three days' time in the Moroccan capital.

Bentley pours himself another glass of rum. They were going to kill someone who had done nothing wrong, and Bentley was responsible for it. Was there anything he could do to stop the execution, or must an innocent man die because of him? Bentley paces up and down in the hotel room wondering what he could do. What time was the man leaving Casablanca? The article didn't say – it could be two in the morning or midnight. He casts his eye over the page again. In small print at the bottom there were some details about the paper; some publishing and distribution information, and the address and phone number in Casablanca where it was printed.

Maybe he can phone the paper and ask the news desk if they know when the man will be leaving prison to go to Rabat. He grabs his jacket and heads out into the old town. Along the cobbled street, through the archway, past the Hofbrauhaus – eventually he finds a public phone. He steps inside and types in the number from the paper. The phone starts to ring. Someone answers the phone and speaks in Arabic.

"Do you speak English?" Bentley asks the man at the Moroccan Times.

"Yes I do", the man replies.

"I wonder if you can help me. I'm a photographer working for Time Life and I've got to get a picture of the man who tried to kill the president of the DRC. I read your story but I don't know what time he will be leaving Oukacha Prison on his way to Rabat. I hope you can give me some information on when he will leave."

"The prison van will leave at ten o'clock in the morning", the voice on the phone tells Bentley.

“Forgive me but how can you be certain it’ll leave at ten?” Bentley asks.

“Because there is only one run to Rabat from Oukacha Prison, and it’s always at ten o’clock. If you want your picture, be outside the prison then. This is the time specified for the Press.”

“Thank you – you’ve been very helpful”, Bentley says in conclusion and hangs up.

So that’s it – they’re taking him to Rabat by prison van at ten on Thursday morning.

“What on earth can I do to stop an innocent man from dying, when it was me who caused this in the first place?” Bentley wonders as he walks pensively back to the hotel.

Chapter 27

When Bentley arrives in Casablanca he doesn't have time for sightseeing. Instead he makes his way along a rather unattractive back street on the east side of town. There he finds the address he was looking for. The man at the counter stands in front of several cabinets which display a range of firearms.

"Morning", Bentley began. "I'm looking for a rifle – maybe a Colt or a Browning."

"We have a good selection of rifles here", the man replies as he points towards the cabinets. "What are you using it for?"

"I'm joining a group of friends to shoot deer in the Atlas Mountains".

The man opens one of the cabinets and brings out one of the rifles.

"This is a Remington Tumbleweed. It's a popular rifle and I'm selling it for only $1800. It comes with telescopic sights, ideal for deer hunting."

"Looks okay – what else do you have?" Bentley asks.

"How about this one", the man replies. "It's a Springfield Nato model, semi-automatic chamber, calibre 308. This one's a little dearer at $2,000."

"Yes I like this one. I'll take it – and some boxes of ammunition. How many in a box?"

"Twenty bullets per box".

"I'll take three boxes", Bentley tells the man.

"That'll be $2,150 altogether, as soon as I can see your permit."

This is going to be an exercise in acting technique and persuasion as Bentley has no permit.

"Have you ever been on holiday and your suitcase didn't arrive with you? That's what's happened to me. My cases have all gone missing, and in them was my licence to use a rifle. I'm meeting my friends this afternoon but they'll have to go on without me if I can't buy a rifle today".

"I'm sorry but I can't sell you a gun without a permit", the man behind the counter replies.

"Yes I understand. It was too much to ask of you. What I was hoping to do was to buy the rifle, and return it to you after I've used it, as I can't take it home on the plane."

"No I can't do it. You must have a firearms permit to buy a gun".

"Oh dear - my friends will be so disappointed. Maybe there's some arrangement we can come to."

"No arrangement. No permit - no rifle."

This isn't looking good for Bentley. The man is adamant and is becoming angered at the audacious request to buy a gun without a licence.

"You know this is holiday of a lifetime and I'm prepared to offer a little extra to make it possible", Bentley says.

"I think you'd better get out of here before I call the police", the man threatens.

"Well you *could* call the police, but then you wouldn't get this, would you?"

He brings out a large wad of notes from his brief case.

"There's $5,000 here. You give me the gun and bullets and it's yours. How about it?

"That's a lot of money – more than I make in four months".

"I don't want to let my friends down, so I'm happy to pay a little extra. No one will know except you and me."

"Well I don't suppose it'd do any harm", the man concedes.

"That's right; no harm at all. Now if you'll put it in a box with the ammunition, I'll be on my way."

The man eventually accepts the money and puts the gun and bullets in a box. Bentley takes it and hands over the cash for the rifle plus the surcharge and walks towards the door.

"You'll remember to bring it back, won't you!" the dealer shouts as Bentley leaves the store and goes out into the street.

There's just one other place he needs to go to before heading back to the hotel – an automotive shop where he can buy a set of number plates for his car.

Chapter 28

It's a long drive from Casablanca to Rabat, but Bentley thought he better check out the road if he were to attempt to hold up the prison van and spring Yassine. Wednesday morning is sunny and warm as Bentley begins his one hour journey along the coast road. He has to look for some ideal spot to stage an ambush; maybe some quiet part of the road, or perhaps a tunnel or road works.

The road is dry and dusty, and busy all the way. To the left Bentley can see out into the Atlantic, and on the right only semi-desert. As far as Mohammedia, about thirty kilometres into the drive, no opportunity presents itself, and it's the main road to the capital, so it will be packed with traffic.

On he drives, looking all the way for a suitable location to stage his attack. Halfway now, and he comes to the toll station at Bouznika. Could this be the place? It would be a very public experience, and there may be police at the toll station. He pays the toll charge and drives through.

He had passed Temara, three quarters of the way into his journey and still no possible place to hold up the prison van. Now he is almost in Rabat. The prisoner would be taken to Zaki prison, north of Rabat in the adjacent town of Sale, and the prison van was sure to take the ring road and bypass the city. Just approaching the ring road Bentley finds the road turns off quite sharply to the right while the non-motorway A3 continues into Rabat. A motorway bridge just past the corner, is out of view of cars approaching. Maybe here? This seems the likeliest place so far. But this isn't a single track country road where he could just force the van into a ditch at the side of the road. This is Morocco's main motorway, and he is on his own.

A slip road takes him off the motorway and onto the ring road, and then into urban streets. Now only a mile from the prison, the road comes to a T junction, and the prison is to the right. After the T junction he pulls over. The street is quiet and narrow. This would be where he'd ambush the prison van and take Yassine. As long as the van came this way, he'd be ready for it. He'd have to take a chance that this was the route it would take. He gets out of the car and looks around. The premises on each side look like old warehouses and depots, all closed down. One car goes past. An old man crosses the road. This is the place.

Back in his car, he drives back down the motorway to Casablanca. Just out of Rabat he starts putting his plan together. He would be outside Oukacha at ten and wait until Yassine was taken out of the prison and put into the prison van. He would follow the van all the way to Rabat and overtake it on the ring road before it turned right at the T junction. A car which he was going to have to steal would be parked on the right after the T junction across from any parked vehicle that was there. He would turn right and drive up to the stolen car, get into it and swing it out across the road so that the van could not pass. Then he'd reverse back and wait for the prison van to turn into the street. When the van had to stop at the stolen car, he'd speed up to the van and pull up behind it. Then he'd jump out of the car and fire two bullets from the rifle through the windscreen of the van and order the guards out. When the guards got out with their hands up he'd shout to them to throw their pistols away. Then he'd point with the rifle to go to the back of the van and open the back door. He'd shout to Yassine to get into the car, and before backing away he'd shoot out the back tyres of the van. He'd reverse back at full speed and swing round at the T junction and get back on the ring road. The guards wouldn't have time to pick up their guns. Too bad if any passing motorist or pedestrian witnessed the scene. They'd better keep away if they knew what was good for them

By the toll station at Bouznika his plan is in place. He heads back to the hotel in Casablanca to rest for a couple of hours then he'd be back in Rabat later in the evening to steal a car. He'd go to the other side of the city and find a car that he could hotwire, or maybe a van, even a bus or a truck. It just depended on what was available when he got there. He'd park it on the street just past the T junction, across from some parked cars, and get a bus or taxi back to his car. The plan was foolproof.

Chapter 29

Those brown UPS vans are easy to steal – especially with the sliding doors and the engine running while the driver makes deliveries. The downside is that the police will be looking for it, but hopefully they won't find it until Bentley has successfully completed his ambush.

After breakfast at the hotel on Thursday he takes a drive across the city to Oukacha prison. He parks the car, now with false plates, and finds a convenient vantage point from the balcony of a high-rise block of flats nearby. He looks down at the heavy prison door through binoculars and waits for ten o'clock.

Some traffic goes back and forth along the road eleven floors below. All seems quiet as he gazes down. A clock nearby starts chiming as ten o'clock strikes. A large navy blue van reverses up to the prison door. The door begins to open and two guards step out with the prisoner handcuffed between them. This is Yassine who is due to die today unless Bentley can prevent it. Bentley catches a brief glimpse of the man's face as he is bundled into the back of the van. It is the same face that was in the Moroccan Times.

The van starts up and pulls away. Bentley gets the lift to the ground floor and walks quickly across to his car. He jumps in and begins following the van through the city at a distance. Beside him is the rifle he will use to hold up the van. The van goes on its way through the city and eventually onto the motorway. All the way Bentley thinks over and over again of how his ambush will go, and if there is anything he might have forgotten or overlooked.

The van passes the turn-off to Mohammedia, with Bentley a few hundred metres behind. His ambush will take place in half an hour. On they continue until they reach the toll station at Bouznika. He watches the van go through. Now it's his turn to approach the toll booth. Suddenly a car seems to come out of nowhere and pushes in, right in front of him. He has to brake to avoid hitting it.

"For Christ's sake!" he mutters to himself.

A hand reaches out from the car in front to offer the payment. Bentley reaches for his money, but the car ahead, instead of pulling away, reverses straight back and rams into the front of his car.

A young woman wearing black spectacles and a beret immediately jumps out, shouting and waving her arms as Bentley looks at her in bewilderment.

"Look what you've done to my car!" she shouts at Bentley.

"Look what *I've* done to *your* car? You reversed into *me*!" is Bentley's angry reply.

The girl goes across to the driver's side of Bentley's car, still shouting and waving her arms about the state of her car. He steps out of his car as the girl comes over.

"Just look what you've done!" she shouts.

"Now just a minute!" begins Bentley, but he is quickly interrupted by the girl.

"It's a trap", she says under her breath. "They're waiting for you to hold up the prison van – they're going to kidnap you. The prisoner's part of the gang."

The queue of cars behind begin a charivari of blaring horns.

"Who are you?" Bentley asks.

"Never mind that now. Meet me in the bar of the Hotel du Paradis, St Tropez, tonight at eight."

Horns are blowing noisily and angry drivers are shouting at the couple.

"You better be more careful in future!" she shouts at Bentley as she gets back in her car and roars off through the barrier.

All the way back to Casablanca Bentley wonders who she was and how could she have known that he was going to hold up the prison van. Now he must quickly make arrangements for a trip to the south of France.

Chapter 30

By the time Bentley arrives at Saint-Tropez the sun is already setting. He makes his way through the town, past the many cafe bars and restaurants along the way. The town has a pleasant atmosphere of people casually sitting outside, sipping Martinis or Camparis and chatting with one another on this warm evening in the south of France.

Just before eight he arrives at the old port where he was to meet the girl in the Bar du Paradis. The harbour is full of boats, from dinghies to cabin cruisers. This is obviously the playground of the rich and famous. At last he comes across the Bar du Paradis and strolls inside. When the waiter comes he orders a Pastis 51 and water.

He gazes out across the harbour as the night grows darker. At least he was about to have a drink with a young woman whom he'd only just met, and he hadn't had to risk his neck holding up the prison van.

"Well – we meet again."

The girl at the toll station is standing next to him.

"Good evening," begins Bentley. "What would you like to drink?"

"I'd like a Mojito please", she replies.

"Let's sit down", he suggests, and calls over the waiter.

He can see that she is a very attractive young woman, but the black spectacles and beret which she is still wearing, give her a rather austere appearance. She has long chestnut hair in loose curls, and her crimson linen shirt is tied around her waist, revealing the curves of her hips. It is deeply-cut at the front, showing her cleavage. Below she is wearing a short white cotton skirt.

"Well – I really don't know where to start. How did you find me on the road to Rabat?" he asks her.

"I was waiting at the side of the road at the toll station. I was watching the cars through a pair of binoculars as they slowed down at the station. I knew you'd be following the prison van, and when I saw it coming I starting looking for a single male behind the wheel.

As you got closer I recognised it was you. I had my lap top set up and when I typed in your registration number, it came up with a different car, so I was sure it was you. Just as you arrived at the barrier I pushed in in front of you."

The waiter comes over with the Pastis and Mojito and puts them on the table with a small jug of water.

"But how did you know I was going to try and spring Yassine?" he continues.

"You called what you thought was a number at the Moroccan Times to ask what time the van was leaving. It was the only call they received, and from a man with a British accent so they knew they could take out the van and that you'd try to intercept it on the road to Rabat."

"You mean it wasn't the Moroccan Times?" he asked.

"It was an office in Kapultski's organisation."

"But I only came across the story of Yassine being wrongly convicted of the attempted assassination by accident when I looked up Lexoplein's website. There was a link to a page in the Moroccan Times, and by chance I happened to notice the story about Yassine."

"It was no accident. When the two agents you overpowered – and may I say in a most imaginative way..."

"Thank you", Bentley says with a brief smile.

"When the two agents found their ID cards were missing, they assumed you'd look up their website to find out more information about the company. A fake web page was set up with the fictitious story of the work the company was supposed to be doing in Africa, and your eye was led down to the column on the attempted assassination. The whole thing was a trap for you to fall in to."

"What would have happened if you hadn't stopped me?" he asked.

"A car was following behind at a distance. The van would have radioed to the car when you held it up, and four men with machine guns would have jumped out, and you'd be thrown into the back of the van".

"It sounds like I had a very narrow escape."

"Yes you did, but I saved you," she assures him.

"Well cheers – here's to rescuing me from who knows what!"

"Cheers," she replies as they sip their respective drinks.

"But how do you know all this anyway?" he goes on.

"A friend who works for the Kapultski organisation overheard their plans for you when she brought coffee to them at a boardroom meeting".

"Who was that?" he asks.

"It was Ramana – Conrad's widow."

"Whose widow?" he asks again.

"Conrad was the man who died in your arms at the cafe in Marrakesh."

"Oh yes, I remember. But why would she tell all this to you, and risk being found out by Kapultski?"

"She found out that Kapultski was behind the killing of her husband, so she set out to find more about their activities, and started listening in at their meetings. She became my friend and confided in me."

They sip their drinks again, as overhead fans blow cool air into the bar. Bentley glances again at her shapely figure.

"And you – why would you go to all this trouble to protect *me*?" he asks the girl.

"I used to work for Kapultski. He told me their company helped poor people in Africa receive medicine, and I believed them until Ramana told me what was going on. I thought you might be able to help us."

"You know, when I look at you I can't help thinking we've met somewhere before," he wonders.

"We *have* met before, Mr Bentley. Don't you remember your first night at the casino in Monte Carlo? I was sitting beside you."

She removes her glasses and beret and lifts her face.

"Do you remember me now? My name is Desiree."

"Of course – Desiree", he says rather surprised and somewhat alarmed at this revelation. "Last time we met you weren't so nice to me"

"I'm sorry I tricked you after you'd so kindly given me your winnings. I've learned a lot since then."

"Well it's all in a day's work for a secret agent", he replies magnanimously.

"Well look – it's getting late now. We've both had a tiring day. Why don't we take it easy and order dinner now. We can go back to our hotels and in the morning we can meet for coffee and plan what we're going to do next," she suggests.

"Sounds good to me," is Bentley's casual reply with another sip of Pastis. "But before then I have to meet an old friend."

Chapter 31

After breakfast Bentley catches a bus east along the Riviera. He relaxes as he looks over the Mediterranean. After a while he reaches Monte Carlo and alights there. He looks around cautiously after getting off the bus before crossing the road towards the casino where he first arrived, what seems a long time ago now. He walks around the back of the casino constantly looking around him. And there she is – just as he remembered her, looking as attractive as ever. He approaches slowly until he is standing right in front of her – a 1965 four litre scarlet Maserati Sebring convertible.

"What a beauty," he whispers under his breath. "Just as I remembered you".

He crouches down on one knee and with a torch and mirror examines underneath. No sign of explosives. He looks around. No CCTV camera. But what's this? Stuck underneath the front bumper he finds a small magnetic unit, maybe some tracking device. He carefully pulls it away from the bumper and gently puts it at the side of the road trying not to disturb it.

He puts the key in the door. He's inside. Now to try the engine. If she doesn't start he's got a problem on his hands, because someone from the casino might be watching. He puts the key in the ignition. The turn-over is slow but there's still some life in the battery. Then she bursts into life.

"Let's get out of here," he whispers, and moves off. He swings the Maserati out of the car park and onto the main road. He heads back to Saint-Tropez with a smile on his face as he enjoys driving his old car again.

After an hour he reaches the hotel in Saint-Tropez where Desiree is staying. He pulls up outside the hotel and goes inside. After a few minutes in the lobby, she appears and greets Bentley with a smile. She links arms with him and asks, "So John, where are you taking me for lunch today?"

"Well I thought Antibes would be a nice place for lunch," he answers.

"Great idea," she says as they walk through the hotel. He opens the door of the Maserati for her and she gets in.

"Wow – what a car!" she exclaims.

"Yes I always did like the classics," he replies and roars off towards Antibes.

She looks casually out to sea as they drive east, with Bentley clearly enjoying the car and the company of this beautiful woman.

"This is the life, Desiree," he says with a smile.

The miles roll by and the Mediterranean glistens in the sun. Yachts and fishing boats are out at sea, and there's a pleasant cool breeze in the air.

When they get to Antibes, Bentley pulls the car over at the side of the road, with the sea to the right and an unoccupied expanse of beach just over the sea wall.

"I thought you might care to join me for a little picnic", Bentley suggests.

"Well yes, that's sounds wonderful, but where will we get something to eat?" she asks.

"I picked up a few groceries after I left Monte Carlo", Bentley explains as he gets out of the car and opens the boot. He gets out a wicker picnic hamper, a carrier bag and a bath towel.

"Shall we go?" he asks as he opens her door.

They walk down to the unspoilt sand and Bentley spreads out the bath towel at a suitable point on the beach. From the hamper he brings out a bottle of Moet and Chandon and two glasses. From the bag he brings out an ice bucket, then starts to take out the plates and cutlery, and from the bag he brings out pate, vol au vents, chicken drumsticks in aspic jelly, celery sticks with a variety of dips, and an assortment of small triangular sandwiches.

"So these are the groceries that you bought on the way?" she asks.

"Well, it's not every day you have a picnic on the beach with a beautiful woman, a classic Maserati across the road, and waves crashing onto the rocks of Antibes, is it?" he replies, as he pops open the champagne. He pours her a glass and then one for himself.

"Your very good health!" he toasts as they clink glasses. "Isn't it nice to be able to relax as if we didn't have a care in the world."

"Well considering some of the experiences you've had recently I'm surprised by your devil-may-care attitude", she tells him.

"Let's put out some of the buffet now", he suggests, and starts displaying the various dishes. They select one or two pieces and sip the champagne as the waves lazily roll in and out.

After half an hour or so, Bentley finally gets round to talking about the maelstrom of events that he has somehow got caught up in. Finding a starting point seems impossible, and Bentley struggles to gather so much information together.

"Why did Kapultski want the President of the DRC assassinated?" he eventually asks.

"Conrad found out that Kapultski wanted to assassinate Marengo so he could stage a coup d'état and put a rebel leader in his place. It would have caused a civil war and hundreds would have died if you hadn't missed the president so that his security was stepped up, and the president-in-waiting, Obooja, didn't get his chance to seize control", she replies.

"Why did Kapultski want to support a rebel leader? Before Conrad died he told me that Marengo was a good leader and that he had the country's interests at heart," Bentley enquires.

"Kapultski didn't care how many innocent people died. He had struck a deal with the would-be president", she continues.

"Why did he want to install a new president? What was in it for Kapultski?" he asks.

"He wanted to get access to the Air Force. He told Obooja he had plans to help the poor people who worked on the land and he had asked him to be able to spread phosphates over the barren land and into the rivers to help the crops grow."

"Kapultski doesn't seem the type to be benevolent. What was behind it I wonder? He told me that because I'd failed to kill the President that he was having to change his plans, and also that now he had some new technology that he was going to use instead."

He offers her strawberries and cream as they ponder what Kapultski might be up to.

"When I got into the plant at Bratislava men were dressed in high protective clothing, and they were incinerating large crates as if they had to completely destroy them. What was in those crates? Were these the phosphates that they going to spread over the land when

Obooja got into power, and if so why were they so dangerous they had to be incinerated so no trace remained?"

"Is it possible," she asks "that what he was going to spread from the aircraft wasn't beneficial to the land at all, and in fact was some sort of poison?" she wonders.

"You mean like Agent Orange? But why pollute a country that has nothing to offer in the first place?"

"Yes I know," she begins, "it doesn't make any sense."

"Where is Ramana now? Is she still working for Kapultski?" he asks.

"Yes, she's working as a maid in his mansion in Marseilles. She heard that Kapultski intends to try again, and he will be having a meeting with some people this Friday. She's going to record the meeting in the theatre to find out what's going on."

"How will you know what's happening?" Bentley asks.

"Ramana's going to phone me as soon as she's recorded something at the meeting, and if we have anything positive to go on, maybe we can let the police know, so they can stop whatever they're planning."

"Good," Bentley replies. "In that case we have three days of having a wonderful time before we need to worry about Kapultski's plans. So shall we have another glass of champagne as we enjoy a day at the seaside?"

"Well we can't do anything until we hear from Ramana, so we might as well relax while we can," Desiree accepts.

"I couldn't agree more," Bentley answers. "Now then, after we finish this lovely picnic, how about we go back to Saint-Tropez for a night on the town?"

"Good idea," Desiree replies with a smile.

Chapter 32

Over the next couple of days Bentley and Desiree live like royalty, with expensive dinners in exclusive restaurants, fine wine and cocktails, and trips into Italy and to the Camargue in the Maserati. The future is uncertain but for the time being nothing is going to stop them enjoying themselves. Desiree had been young and naive to think Kapultski was a philanthropic character, and now she had seen the light thanks to Ramana's information, and Bentley's account of events since he arrived in Monte Carlo.

On Wednesday evening they go for dinner in Menton, the last French town before the Italian border. Tentacles Restaurant is situated on the pier overlooking the sea, and here they say, the finest seafood can be found. They park the car and go inside. The waiter takes them over to an alcove table on the other side from the small band with clarinet, guitar, double bass and drums. They begin dinner with Dubonnet for her and Noilly Prat for him.

The band is playing some light jazz versions of classic songs. When the waiter comes over to take the order, the lady's choice is prawn and avocado cocktail, while Bentley chooses whitebait. For his main course he orders sea bream, while Desiree prefers razor clams and scallops. When the Zinfandel arrives, Bentley soon makes up his mind to leave the car and take a taxi back to the hotel.

Bentley has dressed smartly for the occasion, wearing a dark suit, white shirt and brightly-coloured tie. His companion is wearing a purple satin evening dress and a pearl necklace. They toast each other's good health as 'Manhattan' plays across the room. Although Bentley and his lady friend have been brought together through circumstances not of their own choosing, he finds her conversation quite stimulating, and not at all as he remembered her in the casino the first time they met. She seems to have grown up very quickly since the death of Conrad, and his widow Ramana having become aware of Kapultski's treachery.

As they dine and listen to the band, Bentley can't help but find her extremely attractive. She has the face of a film star, and a voluptuous figure to match.

"What an excellent choice of restaurant", she exclaims.

"Charming, isn't it?" Bentley replies.

"Tell me about yourself", he asks. "Where are from?"

"I was born in Gothenburg and went to University in Stockholm," she says.

"What did you study?" he asks.

"I studied medieval history", she answers.

"And how did you get involved with Kapultski?"

"I didn't have anything to do with Kapultski. When I graduated I was looking for a job in Europe and I found a company in Monte Carlo that was looking for a personal assistant to the director. That was Lafarge."

"Oh yes a lot has happened since then," he reflects.

"It was a good job, well-paid and always exciting."

"What went wrong with it?" Bentley asks.

"You went wrong with it. When you became involved Conrad was killed, and it caused Ramana to seek revenge, and for me to find out the kind of business Kapultski was involved in", she explains. "I had to resign and tell them I wanted to be with my parents in Sweden".

"I'm sorry I caused you to lose your job", Bentley says apologetically.

"After I started hearing rumours about what Kapultski was up to I couldn't have stayed anyway".

By this time the main course has arrived. This has to be the best seafood restaurant on the Riviera, Desiree expresses. The waiter pours another glass of wine each. The band has just begun to play 'Come Fly With Me' when they start their main course.

"And how about you", she asks. "I've never had dinner with a secret agent before."

"What would you like to know?"

"How did you get into it?"

"I was employed by the RAF as an engineer for a few years. A job came up in the SAS so I applied and got it. A couple of years later a job came up in MI6. I wanted an exciting career so I went for it".

"How much have you told MI6 about all of this?" she enquires.

"So far there's been nothing to tell. I need something more tangible, and maybe we'll get that when Ramana phones".

After dessert they have coffee and liqueurs; Tia Maria for her and Benedictine for him. The band has started playing 'La Mer' as a couple get on the floor to dance.

"May I have the pleasure of this dance?" Bentley asks unexpectedly.

"Well," she begins, rather taken aback, "yes, I'd love to".

He takes her hand and escorts her onto the floor. He holds her close to him with his hand on her back as they begin a slow foxtrot so that her face is against his. He can smell her fine perfume as they dance. Bentley finds the closeness of her body very arousing. They have a few more dances to some classic songs, before Bentley pays the bill and asks the receptionist to call a cab back to their hotels. The journey takes about twenty minutes and they chat along the way. They go back to her hotel first.

"Would you care to come in for a drink?" she asks.

"Yes, I'd love to", is his reply.

He pays the driver and they go into the lobby of her hotel and into the lift to her floor. Inside her room she takes off her short yellow velvet jacket and invites him to have a brandy with her.

He takes off his suit jacket and loosens his tie as she makes up the drinks. The room has a king size bed, and at the end of the bed there is a suite area with sofa, table and chairs. Desiree brings over the drinks, but doesn't sit next to Bentley on the sofa. Instead she sits on one of the chairs, with the two brandies on the table in front of them. They propose a toast to themselves and sip the cognacs.

"Well John," she begins, "I've had a lovely dinner, dance and evening, and now all that remains is that we finish our drinks and get ready for bed, which I've been looking forward to all evening. Would you mind helping me with my necklace?"

"No, not at all", Bentley says, trying to hide his surprise, as he stands up and goes over to her. He undoes the clasp of the necklace and she takes it off and rises to her feet. Now at last they embrace with a deep and passionate kiss. Bentley's fingers wander around the evening dress until he manages to undo the zip at the back. The dress drops to the floor. She is wearing matching black lace bra and panties, but also to Bentley's great delight, a pair of black stockings with suspenders.

She removes his tie as he caresses her breasts. With one hand round her shoulders and the other behind her thighs he sweeps her up and carries her over to the bed. As he removes his shirt and trousers, she slips inside the sheets.

In bed they kiss again, sensually and profoundly. Bentley moves down her body, removing her bra, fondling and kissing her aroused nipples. He moves silently down to her hips and removes her panties which she aids by moving from side to side. Her legs apart, he feels her with his tongue, bringing to her an overwhelming sensation of ecstasy. The minutes roll by casually as their lovemaking continues, the only sound being their whispering and sighing, and moving through a variety of positions. From behind he slips his hands under her suspenders and holds her curvaceous hips as they move together, back and forth, lazily at first, then faster until the exhilarating moment arrives where their lovemaking erupts simultaneously in an orgasmic finale.

They lie back down, breathing heavily, his arm around her shoulder, her hand on his chest. Outside the window the waves of the Mediterranean lap against the shore of the Riviera. The occasional car or scooter passes, and old fishing boats knock carelessly at one another.

Chapter 33

The road to Juan les Pins is lined with palm trees as Bentley and Desiree drive into town. In the harbour men are hauling fishing nets and lobster pots onto the quay and people are sitting at tables outside cafes, reading newspapers, or chatting to friends. Bentley pulls the Maserati alongside the harbour wall and switches off the engine. The town is quiet apart from the sound of boats passing and sea birds calling.

"I thought before lunch we might stroll around the town for a while", Bentley suggests as he opens the door for her.

"Yes that would be nice", she replies. "It's a lovely little town, isn't it?"

"I believe there's a little bar around the corner where we can..."

His conversation is interrupted by the sound of Desiree's phone ringing.

"It's Ramana," she tells Bentley.

"Ramana – what's happened?" Desiree asks.

Bentley hears a voice on the phone for a couple of seconds, then nothing.

"Ramana – what is it? Ramana – are you there? Ramana?"

"The phone's gone dead", she says to Bentley.

"What did she say?" he asks.

"She just whispered 'I can't do the recording...I must go', and then she hung up".

"Do you think they're onto her?" he asks.

"I don't know – I can't be sure. Something's gone wrong. She can't make the recording for us. We won't be able to find out what Kapultski is planning", she answers.

"I've heard now from a variety of sources that whatever it is he has in mind will result in the deaths of many innocent people", Bentley says.

"I've heard that too, but we don't know anything for certain. We have no evidence at all that that's what he intends", she replies.

"What if hundreds or thousands of people died, and we did nothing to prevent it?" he asks.

“But what can we do if Ramana can’t make the recording of the meeting?”

“Do you know where the meeting will be held in Marseilles?” he asks the girl.

“Yes I know the house. That’s where I used to work. It’s Kapultski’s mansion on the Rue Géricault. The house is built like a fortress”.

“And the time of the meeting?” Bentley continues.

“Ramana said it’s on Friday at seven”, Desiree replies.

“Can you get us into the house?” he asks.

“Yes – I have a key to get in”.

“And get you get us into the theatre, hidden somewhere?”

“I can get us into the audio-visual room. I can’t record anything but we’d be able to hear the whole conversation”, she explains.

“Then that’s what we’ll have to do. If something’s happened to Ramana, we’ll have to go there ourselves and find out what’s going on. It’s vital we find out what Kapultski’s up to.” Bentley tells her.

“But the place will be full of Kapultski’s men – we might easily be noticed, and if we are, we’re dead”, Desiree warns.

“It’s a chance we’ll have to take. If you can get us into the place, we can hide in the AV room and slip out the back door when it’s over. We have no alternative.”

“I don’t know – it’s too dangerous. We’re sure to be caught.”

“Not necessarily – Kapultski doesn’t know we’re coming. If it was a trap he would have forced Ramana to tell us to come, and they’d be waiting for us at a pre-arranged time and place. I can’t do it alone – you know the place. I’m asking you to come with me.”

Desiree looks out to sea. They could be walking into a deadly situation from which there’s no escape. Kapultski wasn’t a man to mess with. But what had happened to Ramana? Was she in danger? Eventually she realises that she must pluck up the courage to go.

“Okay,” she eventually answers with a deep breath. “I’ll go with you.”

“Thank you. That gives us over twenty four hours. We can stay in my hotel tonight and drive along to Marseilles in the morning. We can check the place over and get prepared for our visit about six o’clock,” he advises.

“I know we have to go but I’m very frightened of what might happen.” she confesses.

“I know you are, but let’s hope we’re lucky and we get in and out safely and get what we want”, he replies.

“I only hope you’re right”, she answers.

“Well that’s settled then. Now – I think it’s time for lunch. Let’s find this little place where they serve calamari and mussels, and a good bottle of Chardonnay,” he suggests.

“Why did you have to be a secret agent? Why could you not have just scraped barnacles from the hull of a boat, or played the violin in some quaint little cafe bar?” she asks with a sense of resignation at what she must do now.

“Well I used to dive for oysters but it was too pearl-less,” remarks Bentley.

No trace of humour is detected on Desiree’s face.

Chapter 34

When Bentley and Desiree reach Rue Géricault it has started to rain. People hurry along the avenue lined with plane trees, reaching in their bags and brief cases for a hat or umbrella. Eventually they come up to Kapultski's mansion. It's a grand, imposing building in a Neo-Classical style with storm-grey stone walls and gargoyles peering down from the roof at anyone who dares to enter below.

"This is the place", Desiree says quietly to Bentley as they stand at the outer gate.

"We better get inside quickly", advises Bentley, "so we don't attract attention."

They go across to the large ornamental black gate and Desiree types in the code number. The heavy gate opens with a loud releasing sound and they pass through. They walk across the courtyard but instead of going up to the front door, they go around the house and come to the tradesmen's entrance at the back. Bentley keeps the black umbrella over them to hide them from the CCTV cameras all around the house. She takes the key from her coat pocket and they are in.

"This way", she directs Bentley as they walk through the corridor. She knows that the cameras are only on the outside of the building.

They walked stealthily through the lower ground floor and up one flight of stairs. She opens a door and they go in.

"This is the remote AV room", she explains to Bentley. "From here we can listen in to the briefing meeting without them knowing."

"It's six thirty now. They should be arriving soon." Bentley says as Desiree flicks a few switches and moves the faders of the mixing desk.

"They won't be able to hear us from here," she tells Bentley.

They wait quietly for twenty minutes until the members of Kapultski's team begin arriving. From the remote AV room the two intruders can hear male voices talking indistinctly as they enter the room. After ten minutes or so the babble goes quiet, and a single voice is heard. It is Kapultski.

"Good evening gentlemen and thank you all for coming. Tonight I'm going to brief you on our African operation on Monday morning. The time will be three o'clock, just before dawn. The place is a mile east of Lashantu, a settlement on the Congo River, twenty miles east of Kisangani."

Bentley and Desiree can clearly hear Kapultski's briefing statements as they listen in. They sit motionless and silent as he continues.

"Two boats will come up the river in darkness. They will stop at an old banana loading area where there are two jetties. Each boat will begin to unload its cargo".

"What *is* the cargo?" Bentley whispers to himself.

"As you all know", Kapultski continues, "we had to change our plans since the failed assassination of President Marengo. We couldn't rely on the use of his successor's air force so we've created our own. Technology has changed since our first conception, both in the product and the transport of dispersal.

This time we'll be in charge of the whole operation without having to stage a coup to overthrow the government. We can run the show on our own without the assistance of some half-wit rebel president."

"How do we get to the location?" someone asks.

"Some of you will be the crews aboard the boats and others will be ground crew helping to unload the drones and standing guard with automatic weapons in case of any trouble. All of us will meet downstream at midnight at a town called Mishunto where we'll pick up the boats. The ground crew will make their way to the location by Land Rover", Kapultski answers.

"Why not just load the drones onto the back of a dozen trucks instead of boats?" another voice asks.

"It would cause too much attention. With two boats we can sail up the river unnoticed, but a dozen trucks might be stopped by the Army", Kapultski explains.

"So that's why they don't need to make use of the country's air force – they're going to use drones instead. But what for?" Bentley again whispers to Desiree.

Suddenly the door opens. Bentley and the girl spin round. A security man in a brown uniform walks in and is startled to find the two there. He tries to pull out his side arm from its holster but Bentley leaps over and with his left hand on the man's forearm, delivers one powerful punch to his face with his right. The man falls back and as he reaches out for support, he hits a switch on the mixing desk. It produces a loud howl of feedback in the theatre.

"Somebody go and find out what's happened", Kapultski is heard to say as the feedback wails.

"Let's get out of here", Bentley tells the girl as the man reels in a semi-conscious state. Bentley hits him again with a microphone stand before pushing him aside.

They run out and along the corridor, down the flight of stairs and head for the back door. It is just in front of them. They open the door and run through. The black gate is ahead. They can do it. They can escape.

"Stop or I'll fire!" a voice screams.

Three armed guards have surrounded them and they have machines guns pointing at them.

"Put your hands up and come with us", one man tells them.

Slowly the two turn to face their captors, as they are lead back to the house. The man reports the capture on his phone. They are taken inside the house and upstairs to one of the rooms. Inside Kapultski sits behind a large desk in a very spacious office.

"Well this is indeed a most unexpected pleasure", Kapultski greets the pair. "How gracious of you to show an interest in my operation. And you my dear child," he addresses Desiree, "we wondered what had become of you, suddenly disappearing without even saying goodbye. After all I've done for you, giving you a good living and money to spend, this is how you treat me."

"Why not let her go? She did nothing wrong – I forced her to come here", Bentley tells Kapultski, trying to get Desiree off the hook.

"How very gallant of you Mr Bentley. You've given me much mirth and entertainment with your tendency to keep popping up in various places around the globe and causing further mischief."

"I'm an agent for the British Government and as such I must caution you that if anything happens to either of us, there will be serious repercussions", Bentley tells him.

“Serious repercussions? Well we certainly wouldn’t want that, would we?” Kapultski replies mockingly. “Take the girl away”, he orders one of the guards.

“Where are you taking her?” Bentley shouts.

“You’ll find out soon enough.”

“She better not come to any harm, or you’ll suffer the consequences”.

“You’re hardly in a position to threaten me, Mr Bentley.”

The girl is manhandled away by two guards.

“Leave us alone”, Kapultski tells the remaining guard. “Mr Bentley won’t give us any trouble, will you?”

The guard leaves and Kapultski asks Bentley to take a seat.

“Well Mr Bentley, we need to find out how much you know, and how much you’ve passed on to the British Government. I’ll be arranging for one of our group to ask you some questions. You may have heard of him. He is known with some notoriety as Abu the Beast”.

Bentley feels a cold shiver at the prospect of being at the hands of this sadistic torturer. He composes himself.

“So Kapultski”, begins Bentley, “it appears you no longer need to overthrow a third world government in order to borrow their air force. Now you can use drones to do it, and launch them from the riverside without anyone noticing. But what cargo is aboard the drones?

“We’ve gone to a lot of trouble since you spoiled our first plan by failing to kill the president. Stupid Lafarge for trusting you to shoot him. We’ve had to rearrange the whole operation. I can’t start giving away confidential information at this stage.”

“Well Kapultski I am flattered. Even now you still expect me to escape.”

“No Mr Bentley you will not escape this time.”

“Well in that case you can answer one or two intriguing questions, such as after you had set up a rebel government in a coup d’état why did you want to use the air force, and why would the new president be happy for you to do so?” Bentley asks.

“It’ll do no harm to tell you now. I wanted to use Hercules planes, often used for famine relief, and so I invented a cock and bull story for Obooja the president-to-be, that as part of the deal of my outfit staging a coup and allowing him to become president, that I would also dump phosphates from planes, just before the rains came to help the poor villagers grow their crops and prevent mass starvation."

"But the fertiliser that you would have spread wasn't beneficial to crop growing, was it? It was the same chemical you were incinerating in Bratislava. It was a deadly poison wasn't it?" Bentley asks. "Why were you destroying it?"

"Well, well, Mr Bentley – you really are a world-class agent. We were destroying it because it was infected and we decided to incinerate it when we found something better."

"What was it infected with?" Bentley asks.

"It was infected with Ebola, spread by monkeys and fruit bats, which as you are aware is a fatal disease", Kapultski answers.

"But you decided there was something better to use and a better way to disperse it?"

"Technology is ever-changing and instead of having to borrow an air force to spread our message, we found a better way – octocopters; eight-engined drones that can carry a paid load of ten kilos each, deliver their cargo throughout the country without being shot down, and when they're out of power they fall to earth harmlessly".

"Why would you want to spread a deadly disease like Ebola on some of the poorest people in the world. What on earth could you gain from that?"

"My view is that I'd be providing a service to the world. People wouldn't have to keep paying up year in, year out for some famine in Africa. The world would be rid of such a burden, and those who die are only worthless peasants anyway. What have they got to be alive for?"

"But why would you go to so much trouble just to kill poor peasants?"

"Well, this is the interesting part of my plan. Firstly I would use my poison to wipe out a million villagers and townsfolk, and then I'd demand a hundred million dollars each from all the developed countries of the world. If a country didn't agree within forty eight hours, I'd unleash it on them and it would serve as an example to the other countries. So you see a hundred million dollars is actually quite a small sum to protect your country from the death of millions of people."

"So that's it – you'd wipe out a million Africans just to show the world you meant business?" Bentley asks.

"The G20 countries would see for themselves the utter devastation caused in Africa, and they would have no alternative but to pay the ransom, or their countries would suffer the same fate as the DRC", Kapultski answers.

"There's one thing you haven't told me yet. If it's not going to be Ebola, then what else?"

"Well I'm an old-fashioned man. I like to do things in a traditional way, and Ebola is too new. Scientists are desperately trying to find a cure for it. What I have in mind will guarantee genocide. It's a disease that has been eradicated all over the world; that is until my team of scientists recreated it. The world has no antidote for it apart from in a few test tubes. They wouldn't be able to produce quantities of vaccine large enough in time. Yes, Mr Bentley; you may have guessed by now – Smallpox."

"My God – you're going to spread Smallpox in Africa? Millions of innocent people will die!"

"The last time we met you gave me a lecture on Pearl Harbour. Now I'm going to give you one on Smallpox. This highly infectious disease has existed for thousands of years. It has even been identified in the mummified remains of Pharaohs. In the twentieth century it was reported to have killed 500 million people. As recently as 1967 fifteen million people contracted it and two million died from it. It was eradicated in 1977, and only exists in a few laboratories for scientific research. But now my scientists have re-invented it. By the time we've spread it throughout the Democratic Republic of Congo, an epidemic of such proportions will travel far faster than a vaccine can be manufactured and dispatched.

All throughout history millions of people have died one way or the other – war, famine, disease. There's nothing new about it. The world needs to be purged to promote the global economy. All I'm doing is taking a fee for arranging it."

Kapultski presses a button on his desk and an armed guard comes in.

"Take Mr Bentley downstairs".

The guard points his automatic rifle at Bentley, and indicates with the muzzle to get up and go with him. Bentley rises to his feet and walks to the door with the guard behind him.

"Farewell Mr Bentley. It certainly has been a delight to speak to a man of principles and intelligence," Kapultski says in conclusion.

As he walks out of the office he tries to take stock of Kapultski's megalomaniacal plan, but he also wonders, what fate is in store for him now?

Chapter 35

His head covered by a hood for sand-bagging, Bentley is taken out of the house and driven for about half an hour to an unknown destination. The engine stops and he is forced out of the car and into some building where two men tie him to a chair before removing his hood. Without a word the men leave the room and lock the heavy door behind them. He hears the footsteps walking away and then there is silence.

Bentley looks around at the room he is being held in. It seems like some sort of workshop, maybe a blacksmith's or mechanic's. The building is like some old, large cellar with no windows; just harsh strip lighting which reveals the cold, bare stonework of the interior walls, and the contents of the room. At one end of the room a forge crackles, full of burning coal embers, with two or three metal rods in the fire. They are glowing red with the heat. Around the room there are steel worktops and benches with an assortment of tools lying on them. There are some hammers, crowbars, pliers and various wrenches. On his right, about three metres off the stone floor there is a pulley with a rope which lies loosely coiled on the floor.

In front of him is an object which he can't fathom. It seems to be a large domed table, with a diameter of about six feet. It looks like a hemisphere made from stainless steel, and a round stem supports it.

Oxyacetylene cylinders for welding stand against the wall, a blowtorch, ropes, rubber tubes, rolls of wire are all part of the strange equipment in this cold cellar vault.

After what must have been about half an hour, Bentley hears voices and footsteps approaching from outside the heavy industrial door. A key turns in the lock and the door is flung wide open. It is Desiree, dressed in a white robe, escorted by two guards. She struggles with them but they drag her across the room.

"What are you doing with her?" Bentley shouts.

They pay no attention to Bentley's question, and drag her over to where he is sitting. One of the men forcefully pulls the white cotton gown off her shoulders and the other one holds her while the gown is removed. She stands naked for a moment, before one man grabs her arms while the other holds her feet and she is forced across the domed metal table in front of Bentley.

"Leave her alone!" shouts Bentley. She shouts at them and tries to struggle. In a minute they have her hands tied separately above her shoulders and bound to the edge of the domed table. She is spread-eagled, with her feet apart and tied to the bottom rounded edge, and her hips forced forwards. The men get up and walk to the door. The door is locked and their footsteps disappear.

"Desiree! Are you all right? Did they hurt you?" Bentley quickly asks.

"I'm all right – they didn't hurt me. They put me in that white robe and forced me here."

She is lying in an arched position facing Bentley.

"What are they going to do to me?" she asks anxiously, trying to move awkwardly on the table.

"I don't know, but don't worry – I won't let them hurt you!" he reassures her.

"What sort of place is this?" she asks.

"Looks like some sort of workshop", he tells her. But now he realises this is no ordinary workshop. Now he realises everything in this room has one common purpose – to inflict pain. Now he realises they are prisoners in a torture chamber – Abu the Beast's torture chamber.

"John – I'm frightened!" she says fearfully. "What's going to happen to us?"

"Don't worry", he reassures her again. "We'll soon be out of here. Just need to get my hands free".

"Listen! Someone's coming!" she exclaims.

They can hear slow, heavy footsteps coming towards the door. Then the rattle of keys and clunking of the lock before the door opens with a loud creak. A tall, heavily-set bald man appears at the door wearing a long black cloak. He stops for a moment then slams the door behind him and locks it. He walks across to where the girl is lying on her back with her groin at the highest point of the arch and her legs apart. Her breasts are pointing straight upwards as her head is tilted back. The man walks across and stands in front of her. He casts his eyes over her naked body, lasciviously.

"Who are you and what do you want with us?" demands Bentley.

The man looks across at Bentley who is tied to the chair with his hands bound behind his back.

"Oh yes," the man begins. "They call me Abu the Beast. You may have heard of me."

"Yes I've heard of you. They say you're a sadistic torturer of innocent people."

"Well, well – is that what they say?

He stands facing the girl and runs his hands up and down her thighs, staring down at her.

"Have you also heard of my special operating table? This is what I call The Mushroom. Let me show you", he says, and reaches for an electrical switch hanging from the ceiling on a long flex. The switch has a joystick which the Beast operates.

"I'll show you what The Mushroom can do", he tells them, and starts operating a few buttons on the switch. He laughs as the domed table is rotated round in a full circle and then is tilted so that Desiree's body can be put into any position. He turns the switch again so that she is made to stand upright, still forced forward by the curved surface. He places her down again at a 45° angle.

"What is it that you want?" asks Bentley.

"What do I want?" replies the Beast. "I'll show you what I want. First of all I'm going to teach naughty girls a lesson that they won't forget, and when I've finished with her, I'll start on you", is the Beast's chilling reply.

"Why not let her go? It's me you want – she doesn't know anything", Bentley explains.

"You don't seem to understand," the Beast tells Bentley. "I don't care what she knows. I'm going to torture her for my own pleasure".

"Oh no!" Desiree cries out. "Help me John!"

"He can't help you – all he can do is watch you squirm as I inflict unbearable pain on you".

"Oh God, no!" she shouts.

"I have a wonderful range of instruments that I've collected over the years", the Beast tells them with a smug smile.

"You must be very proud of your gruesome torture chamber", Bentley says.

"Oh yes, I am, and it'll give me the greatest pleasure to demonstrate some of my instruments."

He picks up a blowtorch and lights it from the forge. It bursts into life. He turns down the flame from blue to yellow and goes across to the girl.

"You better not hurt her – I'm warning you as an agent of the British Government!" Bentley shouts across at him.

The Beast grins as he brushes the slow flame across her thighs. She flinches as she feels the heat from the blow torch. He puts it back on a bench worktop. Next he picks up a pair of crocodile clips with wires running from them.

"This is another idea which I may use on the girl." He holds up the two clips. "Each clip is attached to a nipple, and then a current of a thousand volts is applied. Not enough to kill her, but to amuse me."

"You're an evil pervert", begins Bentley. "What good will that do you?"

"I enjoy the suffering of others, and you – you can sit there and watch everything I do to her."

Desiree lies uncomfortably before the Beast, breathing heavily.

"And then there are my insertion instruments", the Beast continues. He puts on a heavy gauntlet and takes a hot steel rod from the fire. It glows red hot.

"No!" Desiree screams.

"Don't touch her!" Bentley shouts. "I'm warning you!"

The Beast grins as he waves the red hot shaft near her groin. She can feel the searing heat from the glowing rod. Desiree's body is heaving from the anxiety of the threat. He takes the iron back to the forge. He picks up a long cylindrical object now and brings it over.

"Do you know what this is?" he asks Bentley rhetorically. "It's a cattle prod. It can deliver a shock of fifty thousand volts. Can you imagine how painful this would be if inserted here?"

He places the tip of the cattle prod at the entrance to the girl's genitals. Desiree gasps, as Bentley looks on in horror. The Beast laughs and removes the cattle prod.

"No I won't be using these today. Instead I'll be using something more primitive".

He goes over to the wall and picks up a roughly cut, metre-long log with a diameter of about six inches. It has a coarse dark brown bark, with yellow and green lichens and one end has been hacked into a sharp point. He holds it up in one hand so they can both see. In the other he holds a large wooden mallet.

"This is what I'm going to use. I insert it like this."

He places the sharp tip next to her genitals as he had done before.

"With the mallet I hammer the log inside her one bit at a time until it goes all the way up. It's a very slow and painful death", he says leeringly.

"Please no!" cries Desiree.

"If I tell you everything I know, will you let her go?" Bentley asks.

"After I've had some fun with her, you'll be on the Mushroom, and we'll see how much you know."

He operates the switch again and the girl is raised forward.

"But first – why let a pretty little girl like this go to waste. Sit back Mr Bentley and enjoy the show."

He loosens the knot of the long black robe and it falls to the floor. There his ugly, fat naked body is revealed.

"No don't!" the girl screams.

"Leave her alone – I'll kill you when I get free!" Bentley shouts.

"You're going nowhere", the Beast replies.

He stands in front of her naked, his disgusting genitalia in a state of arousal. He begins fondling her breasts and running his dirty hands all over her body as she winces at his lecherous advances. He has moved the Mushroom so he is in a position of easy entry.

"John! Help me!" she screams.

The Beast stands before the girl with his fat gut almost touching her, at a three-quarter angle so Bentley can see what is happening to the girl. Bentley fidgets with the cable ties that bind his wrists. With the fingers of his left hand he tries to tug at a thread on his right cuff. He manages to find it and pulls the thread.

The Beast stands with his legs astride the girl ready to enter her. From the opened cuff Bentley's fingers manage to pull out a razor blade. He holds it between his fingers and carefully puts the blade against the plastic cable tie.

"John! John!" Desiree screams again.

The Beast's sweaty body is touching hers. He is about to penetrate her, but he savours the moment of entry. Bentley swipes the razor blade across the cable tie. It is a difficult angle to be able to cut the tie. Beads of sweat form on his brow as he warns himself silently not to drop the razor blade. The Beast makes leering, lustful sounds just before his moment of penetration. Bentley cuts through the plastic and his hands are free. Just as the Beast is making contact, Bentley springs from the chair, grabs the log that is propped up against the wall, leaps over to the Mushroom and with the log in both hands, attempts to hit him over the head. The Beast catches sight of Bentley and turns sharply and in so doing the log strikes him across the chest. The blow sends him reeling backwards and throws him against a work bench next to the wall scattering bottles and tools all over the floor.

The Beast finds a bull whip on the bench and grabs the hilt. He stands up ready to unleash its destructive power on Bentley. As the whip cracks across the room, Bentley grabs the chair he was sitting on and catches the sharp leather tip around the legs of the chair. He hurls the chair across the room at the Beast and grabs a large hunting knife with an upper serrated edge that he finds on a worktop. Instead of going straight for the Beast, he rushes round to the girl and with one quick slash frees her right hand. He runs towards the Beast, but before he can lunge at him with the knife, the Beast has picked up a heavy crowbar and with a clash of steel the wrecking bar sends the knife flying from Bentley's hand. Desiree has freed her left hand. Now the Beast stalks slowly towards Bentley wielding the heavy steel bar. He crashes it down on a metal bench as Bentley dives out of the way. Desiree has untied her feet. Bentley finds an empty tool box and throws it at the Beast. He ducks again, and moves menacingly towards Bentley. Desiree manages to get off the Mushroom. She finds the cattle prod and picks it up. The Beast approaches Bentley with the steel rod in both hands. Desiree pokes the cattle prod at him from behind and hits his fat buttocks with it. Now the Beast understands what fifty thousand volts feels like as he shrieks in pain at Desiree's assault. He spins round to her. They confront each other. She holds out the cattle prod with both hands and he does the same with the long, heavy wrecking bar.

As Bentley quickly looks around for some other weapon to use, Desiree and the Beast face each other. One blow from the crowbar would kill her for sure. He out-reaches her with the long steel bar, and she has to back away from him to avoid being hit as he swings the bar. They are on the right side of the Mushroom moving away from it. Bentley searches for a suitable tool, such as a sledge hammer or fire axe. But suddenly the Beast swings the bar at Desiree and it brushes against the cattle prod. The bar becomes live and with a scream of pain he drops the bar. Now she has the upper hand. He backs away from her as she thrusts the electric stick towards him. As they advance towards Bentley, with the Beast's back to him, Bentley notices something.

"Desiree – straight forward! Keep walking! Go left!" Bentley calls to her.

She takes a step to her left as she walks forward, directing the Beast with the cattle prod. He glances across but Bentley is on the other side of the Mushroom.

"Forward! Forward!" Bentley calls. "Now straight ahead!"

She manages to lead the Beast towards where Bentley directs her.

"Straight ahead! A little to your left!" Bentley shouts.

The coil of rope lies on the floor, under the heavy metal pulley, and the Beast is heading straight for it.

"Go to your right!" he shouts. "A little more... a little more..."

The Beast looks behind him but can't see the danger ahead until he is upon the loose coil of rope on the floor. Bentley seizes his moment. With one flying leap onto the Mushroom, he propels himself up in the air and grabs the chain which hangs from the pulley. With the rattle of the chain on the pulley Bentley crashes down onto the floor as the rope tightens around the Beast's left foot and hauls him three metres off the ground. He is turned upside down as he waves his arms and right leg in a bid to free himself. It is no use – he is stuck fast, stark naked with one leg tied by the rope and everything else just hanging loose. Bentley quickly secures the rope to a bracket on the wall.

Desiree and Bentley stop dead and look at the peculiar sight hanging above them.

"Well, well", Bentley begins. "This is a side of you we'd rather not have seen."

Bentley finds the girl's white robe and holds it for her as she puts it on.

"Are you okay?" he asks her.

"I'm okay – just a little shaken, that's all", she answers.

“We better get out of here. But first – we can’t leave the Beast to go around torturing people.”

Bentley steps on a step ladder and ties the Beast’s hands behind his back, and looks around at the various objects in the room. He notices the Beast’s little toy with the crocodile clips and wires running to them. He brings the apparatus over.

“I’m going to attach the negative terminal to his big toe”, Bentley tells Desiree as he steps onto the ladder. He attaches the crocodile clip.

“Now then – where should the positive go?” Bentley asks, and after a moment’s temptation restrains himself and attaches it to the Beast’s nose.

This causes him immediate discomfort, but in a minute he will experience much more. Bentley has connected the wires from the crocodile clips to the terminals of the cattle prod, and has put the stunning tool into a vice so the trigger is kept on permanently. All he has to do now is to screw up the vice and the trigger will operate. The Beast hangs awkwardly upside down from the steel girder above the room.

“So Abu the Beast, the world will be a happier place without a monster like you living in it”, are Bentley’s final words as he slowly turns the handle of the vice.

“Let me do it”, Desiree requests. Bentley steps back and the girl starts turning the handle of the vice until it engages. The Beast begins to scream as his body is convulsed with the power delivered constantly from the cattle prod.

“Let’s go,” he says to Desiree as they leave the Beast to suffer his fate until no life is left in him. As they prepare to leave suddenly a sound is heard on the other side of the door.

“Someone’s coming!” whispers Desiree.

“Quick! Hide behind the Mushroom!” he tells her.

As she crouches down, Bentley takes up a position behind the door, armed with a steel tube of scaffolding. The voices get louder and the lock starts to turn. The heavy door creaks open. Immediately the scaffolding bar cracks down on the head of the first guard. Before the second one has time to respond another blow crashes down onto his head. A figure in a white robe runs forward. The two men are lying motionless on the floor. Desiree rises from behind the mushroom.

"Ramana!" she calls over.

It's Ramana in the white robe.

"Desiree! Thank God! Thank God it's you!" Ramana replies.

They hug each other with great affection as Bentley checks the guards.

"Did they hurt you?" Desiree asks.

"The Beast was going to torture me but they decided to start on you first", Ramana replies. She notices the fat, naked body hanging upside down, now motionless. "What happened to him?" she asks.

"His career is currently suspended", replies Bentley, having just met the beautiful slim black woman for the first time.

"Now quickly", continues Bentley. "Get their guns. Put on their clothes and let's get the Hell out of here!"

The women start to pull the shirts and trousers off the men lying on the floor. Once they are well covered with the men's uniforms, Bentley gets the keys to the heavy, creaking door, and they are free.

Chapter 36

Time is short to get to central Africa in time to avert a disaster of global proportions, made slower by Bentley and the two women having to stop off in Morocco to retrieve the rifle that he had secreted there. Behind an old deserted shack somewhere in the scrub, the rifle is found in its case, buried in the sand. As yet Bentley hasn't made any contact with MI6 about the impending catastrophe, and now time is running out. He would have to break the rifle down into as many individual pieces as possible and include various tools in his suitcase to disguise the Springfield automatic and get it through customs at Casablanca and Kinshasa, as well as the two pistols the girls had taken from the guards. From there they would take a domestic flight north to Kisangani.

The flight from Casablanca is difficult with long delays and jostling crowds, but the bustle of travellers helps smuggle the firearms through security. After two hours they reach Kisangani and successfully get through customs again. At the airport Bentley tries to contact MI6 to warn them of the disaster. Now it's almost midnight and they still have to get to Lashantu. The two girls wait, exhausted after such long and gruelling hours of travel. Desiree had just suffered the worst experience of her life, but was brave enough to try and put it out of her mind in order to prevent an international catastrophe. Bentley tries MI6 from his mobile. Finally he gets a signal. The dialling tone rings and he hears a female voice answer. Hurriedly he asks to speak to anyone in authority. He has to waste time trying to find anyone to whom he could warn about the unfolding situation. The lady explains that most of the staff had left for the evening but that an official was available to take messages. He has to try to explain as far as possible of the imminent situation on the Congo River to a man he had never seen or spoken to, only hoping the department would act upon his information The man seems unconcerned and sceptical as if answering one of a dozen daily hoax calls of UFO sightings. Bentley can only hastily give details of the time and place and sketchy information about Kapultski's genocidal intent. In a composed, matter-of-fact manner, the official in London takes down what little information Bentley has to offer, and when the call ends Bentley is left wondering if the official had taken any of it seriously.

"Come on then girls," Bentley says to his two associates. "Let's get out of here. We've got a long way to go yet."

"Did you get through to British Intelligence?" Ramana asks.

"I tried to relate the whole story to an official in MI6; whether he took me seriously is another matter", explains Bentley.

"Don't you have some direct hot-line you can use?" Desiree asks.

"All channels have been jammed – must be a security alert in operation", answers Bentley.

They leave the terminal building and in the car park Bentley's hot-wiring skills come in useful. An old pick-up truck was left unlocked, so he pulls wires down from under the metal dashboard and the engine bursts into life.

"Come on – get in!" he tells the girls, and the three of them sit side by side on the bench seat as they head off towards their destination of Lashantu.

The headlights of the old pick-up peer through the darkness as they bounce along the dirt road. The girls nod off briefly but are soon awakened by the rough-going. So much time had passed and now it is almost two in the morning. Along the way the headlights pick up the occasional glimpse of a jackal or monitor lizard. The drive is hot and dusty, and they have only managed to buy a couple of bottles of water at the airport. Their journey continues and the monotonous drone of the engine is broken by the shrieks of monkeys in the trees above. Hours tiresomely go by until they eventually reach Lashantu. Bentley cruises around slowly fearing Kapultski's men might already be in hiding at the settlement. He finds no sign of anyone. He kills the lights and drives quietly up to the old banana landing platform. The place is dark and deserted. He stops fifty metres away and they get out of the truck, closing the doors quietly.

A crescent moon lights the scene in a pale, ghostly light. There is an old derelict shed next to the ramshackle wooden jetty. Since leaving the airport no one from Intelligence has called back. Bentley is beginning to accept that the three of them are going to have to act alone, without the help of MI6. He starts explaining to the girls what they were going to have to do. From a safe distance away from the jetty Bentley begins briefing the girls.

"It doesn't look like my message got through to MI6", he begins. "We're going to take charge of this situation ourselves if we want to prevent the deaths of thousands or millions of innocent people. It won't stop there – if Kapultski gets his way he'll release the smallpox virus in all the developed countries in the world if they don't meet his demands. This will be the single biggest loss of life since the Second World War."

"What are we to do?" asks Desiree.

"Soon the two boats will come to unload the octocopters carrying the deadly virus. We must storm the boats and prevent them from releasing any of the drones", Bentley tells them.

"How can we do that, just the three of us?" asks Desiree.

"We've never used guns before", adds Ramana.

"I know it won't be easy and that everything's against us. But we must try or be killed in the attempt", Bentley tells them soberly.

"How will we do it?" Desiree asks.

"When the boats arrive we'll hide until they are moored. I'll go to the bow of the first boat and you both go to the stern of the second. We'll jump on board and with the rifle pointing at the crew I'll hold them up. You do the same from behind with your pistols. They'll be taken by surprise but if anyone moves, shoot to kill. We'll round them up in the shed and tie them up with the ships' ropes. We'll get away in the boats and go farther along the river to the next town where we'll get the police to inform British Intelligence".

"You make it sound so easy", Ramana remarks.

"Well maybe it will be", answers Bentley. "Get them to put down their weapons and you can guard the ones on board while Desiree gets them into the shed".

They wait in anticipation as dawn breaks to reveal the African landscape. In the river a group of hippos are bathing. On the other side of the river hyenas chase away vultures as they compete for the carcass of a water buffalo.

"Look! The boats are coming!" Desiree remarks.

"Let's get behind the shed where they won't see us", says Bentley.

They creep out from the bushes and silently make their way to the back of the shed. The boats eerily start to appear through the early mist on the grey river. Their engines have a dull rumble as they approach. Bentley takes up his position on the left of the hut with the two girls on the right. Both boats come into view as they approach the old jetty. They are two small cargo ships with their holds amidships. No one can be seen aboard. Their engines are cut as they come alongside the jetty. As soon as Bentley and the girls are able to board the ships they will spring into action and hold up the crews of both ships.

The boats are almost ready to be boarded. It is almost dawn now and the mist is lifting. With their guns at the ready Bentley raises his hand as a signal to run onto the boat. Steady...steady...But suddenly a group of black armed men in navy blue uniforms appear from nowhere and surround them.

"Throw down your guns!" shouts one of the men.

They look round to see four men pointing machine guns at them. Bentley and the girls reluctantly throw their weapons on the ground in front of them. Some of the crew begin mooring the boats. The leader of the capture party shouts to a subordinate.

"Take the two women onto the boats. We'll pass them round the men and have some fun with them later. Take the rifle and pistols onto the boats."

"The women are under my direction as agents of British Intelligence. If they are harmed you will face serious consequences", Bentley warns the man.

"And you – you will wait here", the group leader tells Bentley. He shouts to one of the men. The man comes over and holds his gun on Bentley. The other three men take the women to the boats.

Bentley can do nothing but wait to see what will happen. The guard continues to point the gun at him as the girls are ordered to get on board. Half an hour passes. The convoy of Land Rovers arrives at the scene and armed militia soldiers jump out. Now it is daylight and the sun is just beginning to surface over the African horizon. Eventually an Army jeep pulls up. A man in uniform has driven Kapultski to the scene.

"Well, well Mr Bentley!" begins Kapultski as he climbs out of the jeep. "You really do have a habit of turning up in the most surprising of places - and how kind; you have brought two lovely young women with you. Just think – all the effort you have gone to has all been for nothing. You'll be able to stand and watch my octocopters taking off with their lethal cargoes, and you can do nothing to prevent it."

"And what about me?" Bentley asks.

"You'll be executed of course", is Kapultski's answer.

"And the girls?"

"Who knows what will happen to them", he replies indifferently.

"It's not too late to stop this now before anyone is killed," urges Bentley.

"You know, far from your constant interference annoying me, quite the contrary – it has positively enhanced the excitement of the experience!"

Suddenly a more serious demeanour descends on Kapultski as he shouts to someone aboard the boats.

"Open the hatches!" he shouts.

The large rusty metal covers over the holds of the boats are pulled open. Bentley watches in anticipation.

"I hope you enjoy the spectacle," jokes Kapultski. "It'll be the last thing you see."

With that remark Kapultski leaves Bentley and strides off.

Bentley stares at the open hatches, as the guard closely watches him. After Kapultski has left the area Bentley hears a shout and then a buzzing sound seems to come from the boats. One by one the octocopters start to rise from the holds of the two boats. They hover for a few seconds until clear of the hatches then start to make their way inland. This is the disaster that Bentley failed to prevent from happening.

Suddenly a shot rings out from one of the boats and the guard holding Bentley falls dead at his feet. He looks up at the boats. The two girls are escaping from the boat, and Desiree is carrying the rifle. As their guard was staring at the ascending drones, Ramana brought her knee up painfully to his groin and Desiree hit him over the head with a wrench she had found on the deck. She seized the rifle which Bentley had brought and with one well-aimed shot, hit the guard in the chest.

Bentley runs over to help the girls off the boat, the air now filled with octocopters on their way to wreak havoc across Africa. They run away from the boat and from the shed, and seek shelter behind the trunk of a fallen acacia tree. They crouch in horror as hundreds of drones emerge from the holds of the boats. All is lost. All this for nothing. Nothing can stop the spread of Smallpox now.

Suddenly over the hills a loud whirring sound is heard. It gets louder until the cause becomes visible. Dozens of Apache military helicopter gunships appear over the hills. The sound becomes deafening as they hover above the escaping drones. Ropes are thrown down and immediately men start to abseil to the ground. A gun battle breaks out between the descending marines and the men on the ground who shoot upwards with sub-machine guns. The marines take up positions on the ground while other helicopters race after the drones. With the strong down draught from their rotors the miniature helicopters are brought to earth harmlessly before they have a chance to disperse their deadly cargoes. As they are driven downwards, the men on the ground hastily capture them and disconnect their power.

Now covers are removed for'ard and aft of the boats to reveal heavy artillery on board. Ack-ack guns start pounding upwards and men on deck continue their machine gun fire. The gunships return fire as do marines on the ground. From his position of safety on the ground Bentley recognises the flag of the DRC on the Apaches. Guns roar from all directions. With the rifle Bentley picks off a sailor on board the boats. The gunships blaze machine gun fire at the boats which answer back with anti-aircraft fire and small arms fire. An Apache is blown out of the sky by one of the guns on board. The soldiers from the Land Rover convoy have taken up position and are firing at the helicopters overhead. The whole scene is deafening and ablaze with gunfire and smoke. Bentley tries to pick off more of the boats' crews while the Apaches continue their task of recovering the small octocopters laden with Smallpox. One man is shot on board and falls backwards into the Congo River. Another helicopter is hit and crashes to the ground. The marines' machine guns strafe the two boats, which answer back with a barrage of blazing bullets.

Most of the octocopters have been driven to earth by the gunships. Firing continues between the men on board with their heavy cannons and machine guns while the marines pepper the boats with gunfire from the Apaches and from the men on the ground.

Bentley and the two girls crouch behind the fallen tree out of harm's way, but he notices some movement in the distance inland from the river. It is Kapultski with the driver in the jeep, heading towards a waiting helicopter which has landed a few hundred metres away and has its rotors turning ready for take-off.

Bentley frantically looks around and sees beside the body of a crew member an RPG 7 hand-held rocket launcher lying by the shore, just along from the jetty. He races through the gunfire and makes it to the jetty to retrieve the missile launcher. Avoiding the hail of bullets he reaches the launcher but stops dead before he picks it up. A four metre crocodile has come out of the river attracted by the smell of blood from the man's body. Bentley stops dead and watches the crocodile waddling over. The RPG7 is between the man and the crocodile. He can't afford to run over and snatch the weapon with such a fearsome sight confronting him. Cautiously he glances behind him. The jeep is almost at the helicopter. He turns back to the crocodile. It has stopped as it chooses whether to go for this quick and easy meal or to take a chance on catching live prey in the shape of Bentley.

Bentley looks behind him again. Kapultski is getting into the helicopter. He spins back.

"Come on! Get a move on!" he shouts impatiently at the crocodile. The monster lumbers forward again and stops. The helicopter is about to lift off.

"Hurry up damn it!" he shouts at the reptile. The crocodile drags its huge leathery body over to the dead man and with a sideways movement with its jaws grabs the body and slowly drags it into the river with a splash.

The helicopter is airborne and heading away from the river. Bentley rushes over and lifts up the RPG7. He places it on his right shoulder and sets the sights to take aim. The helicopter carrying Kapultski is far away now, probably out of range. Bentley steadies himself and focuses on the disappearing dot in the morning sky. He concentrates. He aims. He squeezes the trigger. He fires. With a roar and pursuing horizontal column of smoke the missile flies from the launcher and soars into the sky. He lowers the weapon. He had one chance to get it right. If he missed, Kapultski would start up some other act of genocide somewhere else. The missile blazes through the sky. Will it miss its target or fall to earth out of range? Bentley stares into the sky. He waits...he waits...will the missile catch the helicopter? He waits...A large bright orange explosion in the sky confirms the missile found the target. Bentley has shot down Kapultski's getaway helicopter which starts falling to the ground in the distance. The chopper crashes, its rotors breaking up as it comes to rest. Bentley gives a deep sigh of relief, but it's interrupted by a call on his mobile. An odd to time to receive a phone call, he thinks as he puts it up to his ear.

"Hello?" he asks.

"Ah Bentley", says a male voice at the other end. "Stanshaw here at MI6. I trust everything is under control down there?"

"Well... yes... I think so - the firing seems to have stopped now. I hope the drones have all been retrieved", he answers.

"Yes – the brigadier tells me the operation was a complete success. I think it's all been wrapped up now. Look here Bentley, as soon as you find a hotel can you give me a ring with all the locations and people who have been involved in this whole business. We'll pick them up as soon as we can locate them."

"I'll go back to Kisangani with the girls and get a place there. I'll give you all the information I have", Bentley tells the man from MI6.

"Good show – and then on Monday can you pop along to our office in London? I'd like to have a little chat with you, if you'd be so kind", asks the man.

"Yes, of course - I'll see you then", answers Bentley.

He goes back to the girls behind the tree trunk on the ground. Some men lay dead on the boats while others had been captured. All the octocopters had been grounded before they could release their cargoes. The marines have collected all the drones and are carefully putting them together while they arrange for army vehicles to pick them up. The air is full of smoke but all the gunfire has ceased.

"Well girls", begins Bentley, "looks like it's all over".

"What happened to Kapultski?" asks Ramana.

"His importance was blown out of all proportion", replies Bentley.

"What about the drones?" Desiree asks. "Did they get all of them?"

"All present and accounted for", Bentley tells them.

“Well that’s a relief. When I saw them all leaving the boats I thought it was too late to stop them”, Desiree says.

“Well I think it’s high time we booked into a nice hotel in Kisangani and celebrate with dinner and a few drinks. What do you say?”

“I’d say I’d prefer breakfast”, replies Ramana.

“That’s after a hot shower and a good night’s sleep”, says Desiree.

“Well let’s get the truck and get out of here”, suggests Bentley.

Chapter 37

After several long and luxurious hours at the Leopold Hotel in Kisangani the three accidental heroes finally surface, too late for breakfast but at least they have managed to get a good night's rest at last. Bentley orders a light lunch for three in the hotel restaurant around two o'clock.

On the menu is kedgeree, tilapia, ostrich and a range of exotic fruits. Bentley orders a good bottle of Dom Pérignon to celebrate their success, but also as a farewell drink as they would soon be going their separate ways.

A few tourists and some business people are finishing their lunches in the restaurant of the old colonial hotel. Some music plays faintly in the background as waiting staff in black and white attire attend to the guests who have come to the hotel.

"Where will you go now Ramana?" Bentley asks.

"I'm going back to Marrakesh this afternoon. I still have some friends there, and Conrad's family are living there. I'll be able to find some work in a hotel or a bar", she replies.

"That's good – you'll be with friends again. And you Desiree – what are your plans?" he asks.

"I'll be going home to Sweden today. It's a long time since I was there and I miss my family and some friends. Maybe I'll find a job as a secretary in a company there".

"Well I hope you're both successful in whatever career you choose to pursue".

"And what about you John – where will you go now?" asks Ramana.

"Well I have some personal business to sort out in Glasgow. After that who knows".

"But this won't be goodbye for us. We'll still be friends, won't we?" Desiree asks.

"Of course we will Desiree", Bentley answers. "There will always be a special affection between us."

"After what we've been through together, nothing could keep us apart!" Ramana remarks.

“Very nicely said Ramana”, comments Bentley. “So let’s drink to our reunion, whenever that may be. Let me propose a toast – ‘To the three of us sitting here today; to the adventures of the past, and to the happy times we’ll have in the future’”.

They laugh and clink their glasses, and enjoy their last lunch together, before they have to leave for different parts of the world.

Chapter 38

London on a Monday morning seems like a million miles away when Bentley arrives at an anonymous office of MI6. It is rather a cloudy day, with commuters rushing off trains, and red buses and black taxis carrying passengers to their places of work. As he walks across Trafalgar Square his mind is alive with thoughts of the two girls who had become caught up in this electrifying drama, and what was he to expect when he arrived at the minister's office. Could he be charged with some crime, or in some way held responsible for the events in Africa? Had he trespassed into the uncharted waters of the secret service, and would he now be arrested for acting unlawfully? He had killed Abu the Beast and Kapultski, and others had been killed because of his actions.

The unremarkable grey building of the secret service to which he has been directed looms above him as he walks through the front door. The commissioner at reception asks if he wouldn't mind waiting for a few minutes until the Minister was ready.

Bentley sits in an old bottle green leather armchair, and looks around at the lavishly decorated interior. A marble staircase leads to offices upstairs, and rooms are adorned with elaborate cornices and wood-panelling. He sits apprehensively for several minutes, until the commissioner speaks to him again.

"The Minister will see you now Mr Bentley. Please go to room eighteen on the first floor."

Bentley thanks the man, and begins to ascend the marble staircase. In the corridor are portraits of unknown dignitaries from the past. He arrives at room eighteen and knocks on the door. A voice from within invites him to enter.

"Mr Bentley – do come in", a man says from behind a large Victorian desk. "Please have a seat – good of you to come. Edward Stanshaw".

He offers his hand to Bentley who replies, "I'm very pleased to meet you".

Stanshaw sits behind his desk again and presses a button on the intercom. "Bring us some coffee please Cynthia, if you'd be so kind."

"Now Bentley I've asked you here today to discuss with you the events of the past few weeks. I can give you an update on the situation since you phoned from the hotel. We've been to all the locations you told us about, and we've spoken to the people involved. All those who worked for Kapultski are behind bars now, including those in Madeira, Marseille, Bratislava, Helsinki and Monte Carlo. We've also interviewed Fiorenza, Angelo, Tupelo Joe, Ramana and Desiree."

"They had nothing to do with it," Bentley interjects. "They were only trying to help me."

"I'm aware of that Mr Bentley and as such they will face no charges, and furthermore, neither will you", replies Stanshaw.

Bentley seems relieved that neither he nor those who had helped him were not to be charged with any crime. He sits back in the chair with a breath of relief.

"Mr Bentley, you have averted one of the worst catastrophes in modern times. Quite how you got involved in all this is something of a mystery, but none of that is important now. All that matters is that millions of lives and billions of dollars have been saved by you, almost single-handedly", continues Stanshaw.

"Well it was just something I seemed to wander into", Bentley replies vaguely.

"Now all that remains is for me to offer you a little compensation for all the trouble you've gone to".

"Compensation for me?" Bentley asks, rather surprised.

"Yes. Fiorenza, Angelo and Tupelo Joe are each to receive full citizenship in Britain and the United States, plus an award of £50,000 each", Stanshaw reveals. "Desiree and Ramana will be awarded half a million pounds each."

"Why that's wonderful!" Bentley replies. "Now they can start a new life and buy some things they want. Fiorenza can buy herself some nice dresses and jewellery, and maybe Tupelo Joe will take up singing again."

"But for you, we have a special gift of ten million pounds tax free, with most of the developed countries contributing a sum of money as they would have had to spend many millions more than that if Kapultski had succeeded."

"Well I'm astonished! I didn't expect any reward."

"Oh by the way – one last thing. President Marengo of the DRC wishes to thank you for saving his life, and asks if you wouldn't mind attending a banquet in your honour at the Presidential Palace in Kinshasa".

"I'm lost for words...I would never had imagined..."

"Well I think that's everything. I'll be in touch about the transfer of funds etcetera, but meanwhile thanks for coming, and good luck. Oh by the way, this comes under the Official Secrets Act now, so don't mention it to anyone, there's a good chap."

Stanshaw stands up and shakes Bentley's hand. Bentley thanks the minister in a rather stupefied way, turns and walks out. He needs fresh air; he needs to compose his thoughts; he needs to get to the Duke of York quickly for a large gin and tonic.

Chapter 39

The silver hired Ford Focus cruises through the streets of Glasgow. Bentley passes some of the places he used to know. On the left he sees the Horseshoe Bar where he used to drink. A little further on he passes his old bedsit above Kebabylon. Farther still he glances at Cleopatra's Asp, the nightclub all closed at the moment. Eventually he turns the corner and passes The Squid Squad chip shop. He stops the car and switches off the engine outside an old run-down tenement that he'd visited before.

He crosses the road and enters the close. He walks up the stairs and is confronted by a man outside one of the flats.

"Get out of my way", Bentley tells him.

"Hey! Who d'you think you are? You can't go in there!" the man replies.

"Just watch me", is Bentley's answer.

The fat, sweaty bald man with a gold chain round his neck tries to block Bentley's entrance to the flat. In a second Bentley has the man's arm twisted behind his back.

"Take a walk or I'll throw you down the stairs", Bentley warns him.

"Okay! Okay! I'm going!" the man shouts.

Bentley releases his grip and the man runs down the stairs and out of the close. With one almighty kick Bentley breaks open the front door of the flat and walks into the bedroom. A girl and a man are in bed together. The man tries to get out of bed quickly.

"Get your clothes on and get out!" Bentley orders.

"Who are you? I thought this was a safe house!" the man shouts back.

"For you it's a dangerous house if you don't get out of here now", Bentley replies as he grabs a bundle of the man's clothes and throws them at him. The man grabs all the clothes, his socks and shoes, his trousers, and runs out of the flat.

"What do you want?" the girl asks.

"Don't you remember me?" he asks with a smile. Suddenly a broad beaming smile greets her face. It is Zoulla.

"You've come back!" she excitedly replies.

"I'm taking you away from here. Get your things", he tells her.

Just then two heavily built men appear at the door. They are a pair of scruffy, overweight bruisers, sent to deal with Bentley's uninvited visit.

"You're in deep shit now, pal", one of the men says as he produces a knife and flicks out the blade. Bentley starts to twist the button on his right shirt cuff with the fingers of his left hand. Suddenly a twin-barrelled derringer flies from his sleeve into the palm of his hand. He holds forth his outstretched arm.

"Now who's in deep shit?" Bentley replies with a smirk. "Drop the knives!" he orders. The man throws his knife down.

"Now yours!" Bentley tells the other gangster, who pulls out a knife from his pocket and throws it on the floor.

"Turn around and put your hands on the wall!" he tells them, his back towards the open door. A figure appears at the door. It is the pimp in the gold chain who had been guarding the door.

"Look out behind you!" Zoulla screams.

Bentley spins round but the nearest man quickly catches Bentley's right arm and in a second has him immobilised in a full nelson with the thug's hands clasped behind Bentley's neck. The first thug removes the derringer from Bentley's hand.

"We gotcha now, big man" the first thug tells him. "Now ye're gonna get it!"

The other thug keeps a stranglehold on Bentley while the first one picks up his flick knife from the floor.

"Gie him it in the belly!" the second one shouts as the first prepares to stab Bentley in the stomach.

Suddenly three shots blast out in quick succession. Zoulla has got a gun. She has shot the man holding the knife, and he drops to the floor. The second man throws Bentley to one side and runs down the stairs. Zoulla runs after him and on the stairs fires three times. The man sprawls head first down the stairs. The pimp has made a run for it and has gone into the street. Zoulla runs past the man on the stairs and goes after him. The man is running along the middle of the road. Zoulla, in just a scanty nightie, stands with feet apart and both arms outstretched with the Luger in both hands. She fires - but misses. He gets farther away. She has one bullet left. She focuses. She aims. She fires again. The second shot stops him dead.

"Let's get out of here!" Bentley says, now beside her in the street. They run across to the car. He opens her door and she gets in. He jumps in and roars away from the scene.

"Keep the gun", Bentley tells her. "We'll wipe the prints and throw it in the Clyde. Where did you get it?"

"A gangster left it behind by mistake", she explains.

The Ford races away through the streets of Glasgow. Bentley heads for the M8 eastbound.

"Where are we going?" Zoulla asks.

"Manchester airport", he replies.

"What are we going there for?"

"To get out of the country", Bentley tells her.

"But I've got nothing to wear", declares Zoulla anxiously.

"In the bag on the backseat you'll find some clothes, some toiletries and make-up", he tells her.

"But I have no passport", she states.

"When we stop at Tebay a hundred miles from here I'll take your picture and email it to the Ministry. By the time we get to the airport someone will be there to give me your passport", he explains.

"A passport just like that?" she asks.

"I got it fast-tracked for you", he tells her.

"How could you do that?"

"All in good time, Zoulla – all in good time."

Ten minutes later the Ford takes the turn-off to Carlisle, heading for the M6. Zoulla looks out of the window in disbelief at what just happened, but wonders what's going to happen to her now?

Chapter 40

La Confiteria Ideal has to be the most characterful of all tango salons in Buenos Aires. Its sumptuous chandeliers and decorative pillars give a haunting sense of mystery and charm which is never quite felt in any other salon. Bentley has brought Zoulla here as a surprise, and they have a table beside the band in this classic venue of tango.

They sip margaritas as they watch the tangueros glide silently across the floor to the melancholy music of the bandoneon, violin, clarinet and double bass. Zoulla looks attractive again in her elegant purple dress and make-up.

"I can't believe it! A real tango salon in Buenos Aires! You freed me from my life of misery and brought me here – why would you do that for me?" Zoulla asks Bentley.

"Everybody deserves a nice holiday once in a while", Bentley answers.

"But I don't even know you. I only met you for a minute, a few months ago. I don't even remember your name."

"It's John – John Bentley", he replies.

"Why would you go to all that trouble to get me out of that awful place with those vile people?" she asks.

"Sometimes you need a helping hand to get out of the gutter", he tells her.

"But I'm nothing to you... or to anyone".

"You showed me the way to get back on the right track, and now I'm doing it for you", he answers.

"I don't understand – nobody's ever been kind to me before. Why should you?" she continues.

"It's about time you got a lucky break", he tells her.

Dancers circle around the floor, the men seemingly dispassionate and stoical while the women perform strangely sensual moves, twining their legs seductively around the man as he holds her close to his chest. The sombre music creates a profound and moody atmosphere in the historic salon.

"I remember some of the things you told me. You had lost your job, your mother was dying and your wife had a lover. Isn't that right?" she asks him.

"Well remembered; that's about it", he answers.

"And wasn't she going to try to get all your money?" she persists.

"Yes it's true. She accused me of adultery and was going to divorce me and get the money my mother left me, although she was the one who'd been unfaithful. But suddenly the tables were turned. I remembered that I had installed a hidden camera in the bedroom in case anyone broke in and stole my computer which had my novel in it."

"Oh yes – you were writing a spy novel", Zoulla remembers.

"I found evidence of my wife and her fancy man having sex in the bedroom, with the date, time and incriminating footage", he explains. "That'll ensure she won't get a penny now."

They order two more margaritas as they watch the dancers on the floor.

"It's almost nine o'clock". Bentley tells her.

"What happens at nine o'clock?" she asks.

"The band are about to play a special tune which I'd asked for", he replies. "May I have this dance?"

They go onto the dance floor and the band begins playing the song that Bentley requested for nine o'clock.

"Do you recognise it?" he asks.

She is silent for a moment as she listens to the haunting tune.

"It's the song I used to dance to with my father", she replies, her eyes welling with tears again.

Bentley holds her closely and they start to tango slowly around the floor of the old salon. She rests her head against his chest as they move without speaking, under the chandelier, through the pillars. Zoulla's troubled mind enters into a trance of tranquillity as she listens to the beauty of the music. She remembers her father as they dance, and feels a mixture of joy and sadness as she reflects on the path which her life had taken. The moving song ends and they return to their table.

"Thank you Zoulla. It was a pleasure to dance with you. Oh by the way – I almost forgot. The Home Office called me this morning.

They have found your mother and sister. They're alive and well." Bentley takes her hand as he breaks the news.

Zoulla's face goes cold as she sits expressionless for an indeterminable period of time.

"They found my mother and sister?" she eventually asks in astonishment. "How are they? Where are they? How did you manage it?"

"They're here in Buenos Aires. That's why we came here. When you lost them at the harbour they eventually managed to stow away in a container ship, and this is where it took them. Tomorrow you'll be able to meet them", Bentley tells her.

"You found my mother and sister! They're alive! I can't believe it! I just can't believe it!" Zoulla repeats. "We're meeting them tomorrow? Is it possible after all these years?"

"I thought you'd be pleased", says Bentley with a smile.

"Pleased? I'm...I'm speechless!" Zoulla exclaims excitedly. "You've made me so happy! I just can't believe it! You're just so amazing! You're incredible! You're...you're just such an unbelievable hero!" she declares as she throws her arms around his neck and kisses him on the cheek.

"Me a hero?" replies Bentley nonchalantly. "I'm just an ordinary kind of guy."

15957670R00088

Printed in Poland
by Amazon Fulfillment
Poland Sp. z o.o., Wrocław